# THE WARD

(A Crime Novel)

By
Adrian Griffin

For Sherry

PROLOGUE

What struck many witnesses to the event - one of
the competing sensations in the next day's papers -
had been the young man's "wild and crazed eyes" and
"erratically violent behavior."

The news outlets sold a lot of papers that day —
and would for days to come. Far more than they
would've moved with, yet another somber report on the
ever-mounting death toll a historic heat wave was laying on much of eastern Canada and the U.S. the past
two weeks.

It was early July of the first year of the 20th cen-
tury and the humidity of late summer had already arrived, the vanguard to the daily heatwaves. The city
sweltered under the oppressive morning heat that only
promised to climb throughout the day until the evening's all too brief respite.  It was always said in the city
that heat like this brought out the beast and madness
in people and, to many, the day's events merely con-
firmed the adage.

The young man had thrown himself against the
large, heavy oak doors of City Hall then barreled into
the street, leaving in his wake confused and disgruntled citizens whom he'd either bowled over or frightened out of his way. The effect wasn't because he was
particularly fit or imposing in stature but that his behavior was so frighteningly unpredictable.

It was observed that the young man seemed of
good family, he was well groomed with a fine set of

clothes, although he wore no hat, his collar was askew, tie undone, and waistcoat unbuttoned. His clothes also clung to him as if he'd just stepped out of the tub and had dressed without drying. As one citizen put it, he was "sweating like pig – and a sick one at that."

He was a man grasping and clawing for breath, completely unaware of his surroundings or the effect he had on those he passed. In short, he looked like a mad man.

After crashing into the street, he had sprinted east along Queen, almost daring those who crossed his path to confront him. The people of this polite city, though, wouldn't keep his gaze, let alone brave a confrontation.

Crossing Yonge, he'd paused as if to breathe in his surroundings, to take account of... something. Then flashing a brief look behind him, seeing or not seeing, he suddenly spasmed as if he received an electric shock, something striking fear into his soul and turned to run north, knocking those aside who blocked his way.

Heading east again, and passing Massey Hall, the city's new concert venue, renowned for its acoustics but now, bearing silent witness to the day's event. At the next crossroads, he slowed, stopping to gaze at St. Michael's church.

He stood, as if in a trance, licked his parched lips, drew a hot breath through his nostrils and eyes rolling up in their sockets, wavered there. Those who glimpsed the moment of this now limp and frail stance, swore it looked as if the slightest breeze blew him to and fro.

The clanging bells of two passing trolleys and the distant sounds of people yelling to catch a ride snapped him back into the present and prompted him to head south towards the expansive lawn that surrounded the massive Metropolitan Methodist church.

The greensward, with its towering maples, was a popular spot for workers on lunch-break wishing to take some air after working in their stifling, sweaty offices, and Mr. Eaton's garment factory nearby. A couple of hours from now it will be packed. Today, though, there'd be no comfortable lunch, folks tucking into their cold-cuts and pickles.

And at this hour of the morning, few would have noticed the young man nervously striding across the lawn, his attention fixed on the entrance to the church.

*

It had been one of the young ministers who first noticed what he'd later call "some dark blur" rush into the church. He'd been in the vestibule with a small group of parishioners discussing a clothing drive for the area's more needy children. Though momentarily distracted, he soon returned to nodding the requisite times to the group's unremarkable questions. Being insincere while seeming so was a trait he would carry through his entire career and later, while dying of alcoholism, he would wonder if the boredom he felt listening to the sanctimonious had helped give him his deep and gorgeous thirst.

A moment later, a glance down the aisle indicated that the dark figure had made its way to the pulpit. Confused, the minister now assumed it was one of his brethren and, again, went back to his conversation. It wasn't until he began to hear some strange muttering - or what he thought could be chanting - that he decided he'd have to intervene.

"I say, who's there?" he called out, taking a tentative step toward the aisle.

"Is that you Marshall?"

There was no response from the figure which had made its way under the choir loft where, what little light that made it through the stained-glass windows, was further diminished by the overhanging balcony. No way of telling who it was.

The minister excused himself from his party and started towards the pulpit. Perspiration had begun to form on his brow, and he became aware of his heart pumping with such force that he had to stop.

Looking back, his party watched him attentively, curious as to what action would be taken. He then pressed forward, searching in the dim light. His voice, now shaking slightly, suddenly blurted:

"Listen, if this is some joke, sir, I'll have to call for the constabulary and have you…"

The minister had got to within 15 feet of the young man when, yes, what he had heard was definitely chanting. But not in English or any other language the minister understood. He had studied French, Latin and some German in high school and, once he was in the seminary, more Latin. This intoning, however, stumped him.

Whatever it was, the voice resonated throughout the church as a wave of sound as indistinct as the figure itself. Years later, he would remember there'd been nothing in all his training that could have prepared him for anything like this. Here was a human being, a person lost and in pain, yet now, all the catechisms and all the teachings seemed somehow pointless, ludicrous.

Sensing the judgmental eyes of the parishioners on him, the minister took another cautious step.

"Again, I say, I'll have to call on…."

At that, the man, clearly distraught, turned on him, eyes wild as a rabid dog's, tears streaming down his face mixing with already drying sweat.

His face was ashen, save for the dark circles under the eyes, and an intense stare, imbued with overwhelming nervous tension, stopped everyone dead.      Abruptly, the man wheeled to face the great organ pipes that rose up the rear wall, threw up his arms, with his fingers, fashioned what looked like a triangle.

He was now fuming, almost howling, spitting out venomous-sounding words no one could understand. It was as if this lonely, forlorn figure had somehow become a demon here to bring down this house of God.

Arms still upraised, he spun to face his onlookers, a manic glee in his eyes. The minister and parishioners reacted with a start, the minister almost checking to see if he pissed himself.

Just as suddenly, the young man dropped his arms, closed his eyes, slumped his chin to his chest and began quietly mumbling to himself.

For a full minute, maybe more, nobody moved. Time hung suspended.

The minister took a deep breath to recover some courage. He stepped forward and, as he did, the young man snapped his head up staring directly into the minister's eyes. There was a hard resolve in the young man's face, cold, utterly devoid of emotion. His life crushed out of him.

As the minister, readying to say something, slowly extended his arm, the man pulled a revolver from his jacket pocket, placed it to his temple and pulled the trigger.

The sound of the shot echoed through the empty church as parishioners dove for safety while the minister, ears ringing and temporarily deafened, could only stand staring at the horror that had just unfolded. In unknowing shock and shaking his head from the pain, he forced himself to look. He had never seen death close up, and it would change him.

He could sense the panic, heard the muffled screaming as people fled for the open doors, afraid the revulsion laying there, with only half a face staring back, would somehow rise to murder them.

With confusion and screaming all around him, the minister continued to stare, mouth agape, at the lifeless body.

*He was about my age. Why? What could be so bad? What?*

CHAPTER 1.

Was it the pounding in his head or the knocking at the door that had brought Ifan Davies back from his dream world. *What day of the week is it?* He'd lost track.

Still not fully awake, his hangover was kicking in and felt like it would split his head in two, clouding his every thought.

Slightly opening his eyes, he winced. A dim light slipped through a threadbare curtain that fluttered lazily in a hopeful breeze but brought no relief. *Morning,* he thought, and wrapping a shirt around his head to block out any light, started to fall back asleep.

"Sir... inspector Davies?" said a voice, far off in a fog, again with an insistent knocking.

*A hallucination?* He wondered, struggling to get back to his dream where he would see her again.

*

He was standing as a young man in the middle of Elizabeth Street waiting for someone. He couldn't quite recall just who he was supposed to be meeting, but the memory was slowly building as he gabbed with Vince, an Italian butcher some few years older than himself.

The conversation wasn't making any sense, just Vince's meaningless chatter filling the air. Ifan couldn't care less. He was waiting for someone and excited about it.

Out of the corner of his eye, he caught sight of a flash of yellow, a flowing skirt and a shock of black hair, a face upturned to the warming sun. His heart jumped. He reached for his packet of cigarettes, had one to his lips and lit in one fluid motion, then caught his reflection in the butcher's widow. He was pleased with what he saw - young and strong, the requisite gangster looks and a hard-on of anticipation for the encounter to come.

"Yeah, thanks Vince, gotta go."

And with that, flicking his cigarette to the gutter, he was off towards the yellow dress.

"You came," he said with a beaming smile.

"I said I would," said the woman with the most striking blue eyes.

"Yeah, you did."

Ifan stepped closer, into the scent of some kind of flower in her hair he couldn't recognize, then he reached out to…

"I was sent…" interrupted the voice again, … "inspector McCloud needs…" the voice from behind the door continued, snapping Ifan unwillingly back into the present.

He instantly hated whoever was on the other side of the door. He hated that he'd brought him back from his memories.

*We were so young then. I wonder what she'd be like now. Where would we be?* These thoughts swirled as Ifan came back to the world.

"Sir, I'm sorry, it's constable James… ah, constable Jimmy Donahue."

*Ugh, he just won't go away.*

Davies lay still, the dirty shirt wrapped around his head, listening to his unwanted visitor. He was far and away, near and gone, without body but full of pain. If the voice would just stop talking and knocking, his desire to punch him in the face would subside to plain hate.

It wasn't that he was hung over so much but shattered. That particular state of a man trying to obliterate the self and all memory of a life, yet not die because he liked to feel his pain, to swim around in his own bowels and filth because that's what he believed he deserved.

Laying there half-naked and sweating on his, doubtless, bug-ridden mattress. He could hear the constable's words, but understanding was far harder.

CHAPTER 2.

An hour earlier, Inspector William McCloud of the Metropolitan Toronto police stepped from his carriage shielding his eyes from the morning sun that hung low and seared down Queen Street, blinding him. *Jesus Christ this is gonna be another scorcher of a day*, he thought. *Thankfully* he'd put on fresh underwear.

There was a fair bit of peacock to him. At six foot two, proudly bearing profuse, well cared for, strawberry blond whiskers flowed about a prominently jutting chin. Wavy, shoulder-length ginger locks lent him a strangely feminine vanity that was incongruous with his deep-set, coal black, cruel eyes.

With little effort and few words, McCloud was able to create great unease in those he met, an ability unique to a special kind of policeman. Many a visitor to a holding cell or interview room had freely given up information to avoid whatever they perceived to be on the other side of those eyes and their malicious dancing.

His manner and style of work, he liked to think, was straightforward and plain talking. His generation, unlike this new breed of policeman, reformers, and do-gooder politicians, wasn't afraid to crack some heads if necessary. The younger generation, he couldn't help but think, were spoiled and soft.

McCloud lorded over his division as if it was his own little fiefdom, barely hiding his contempt for his superiors. What some called insubordinate, he called *getting things done*. Nobody would openly challenge him.

He was feared for many reasons, not least of all for his sadistic humiliation of subordinates, who he liked to maintain power over to do his bidding. He was also very well connected politically.

On this day, he wore a lightweight, stone-coloured suit with tan boots and straw hat, cutting the figure of a young man strolling at a garden party, not that of a weary 50-year-old inspector making his way to the scene of a suicide.

He blustered his way through the throng of news-papermen scrounging for any morsel they might add to their stories, kicking at one who had dared get in his path. *Damned bottom feeders… a pack of street dogs.*

The press seemed to have doubled their interest in newly formed detective branches that had been em-ployed not just in Toronto but around the world. There was money to be made in gruesome headlines and ce-lebrity detectives.

The public's appetite for murder and stories in-volving the work of these detective squads had reached a fever pitch after the Whitechapel murders. Although McCloud secretly enjoyed his new-found sta-tus, he still viewed the press with suspicion, if not con-tempt.

As he approached the entrance to the church, his eyes took in all that surrounded him, collecting images, impressions. More immediately, he'd have to deal with the young constable bounding down the steps towards him.

The officer had been consoling a group of parishioners in various degrees of shock. Some simply sat
slumped on the steps, staring blankly across the lawn.
Others were hyperventilating, whimpering, moaning,
some still screaming. Police were all about, trying to
calm them, trying to take statements. A few others had
been charged with keeping the gawkers and press
from entering the church.

"So, who are the wailing cats, Jimmy?"

McCloud gestured with his chin; his hands deep
in his pockets. He'd also purposely stopped short, so
constable Jimmy Donahue had to make extra effort to
get close enough to hear him. This manipulation was
another technique McCloud would use to unsettle subordinates and establish a measure of control.

"Mmm…parishioners, sir. They were in the
church when the deceased blew his head off."

Donahue enjoyed the sensation of getting out a
forthright answer.

"Blew his head off? What? You mean suicide?"

"Yes, sir."

Head bowed in thought, McCloud stared at his
boots and kicked at some loose pebbles on the walkway. He knew what was waiting for him, these things
were never a pretty sight and although a seasoned vet-
eran, he delayed. Pulling out a handkerchief to wipe
the inner band of his hat, he took a deep breath and

exhaled in a sigh. Finally, he motioned the constable to head towards the entrance.

"Well go ahead, best show me."

It took several moments for their eyes to adjust to the dimly lit church. Everything inside was a shadow, black with no definition to the expansive room caused by the momentary change in light. A dark figure was sitting in the front pew, and the outline of a constable who was standing guard over something on the pulpit.

Moving down the aisle, McCloud could begin to make out the figure sitting on the pew was a young man who seemed to be talking to himself, shaking his head from side to side. What he was saying was inaudible. It could have been prayer, being a church.

"Are you alright, son?"

McCloud barked for effect, startling the minister to his feet. The minister reeled about to see two figures approaching but they were back-lit from the entry way, and he couldn't guess which might have spoken.

"Fine thank you…who's asking?"

"Inspector William McCloud is who."

"Inspector, sorry I was just…. I'm the minister here. I was here when the…"

His voice began to trail off as he looked slightly over his shoulder.

Laying under a coat, a makeshift shroud, was the body, a pool of blood forming around the head.

"I suppose you'd like to see the body," said the minister, with a habitual politeness.

"Yes, that'd be helpful." McCloud shot back sarcastically and pushed past the Minister.

The guard stepped back.

Squatting over his heels, McCloud peeled back an expensive tailored jacket, not a coat as he'd first thought. His systematic mind next noted that the suicide was right-handed.

The bullet had entered the right temple where the flash from the muzzle had burnt the flesh, exposed a small hole, then exited through the back, left side of the skull creating a much larger and pulp-like wound. The force of the shot had staggered the man backward to where he lay, remarkably gun still in his hand.

McCloud then searched the victim's pockets, again taking in that the suit was of very high quality. Peeking through the lapel buttonhole was a small white gardenia, crushed. A gold watch and chain with fob stretched across a velvet waistcoat with satin lapels. There was also the distinct odor of eau de toilet and hair pomade.

A quick perusal of the deceased's hands and nails revealed a lack of callouses and an expensive manicure, denoting a life spent in drawing rooms not heavy lifting.

"Donahue!"

McCloud had shouted over his shoulder, not looking back as he continued his examination.

"Has anyone out there been able to identify the deceased?"

Stepping forward, Donahue drew out his small, black notebook, flipped to the page he wanted and leaned towards the inspector.

"A Mrs. Johnson, who is part of the parish planning committee and was witness to the suicide along with the minister here and others of the commit…"

The inspector, irritated, stood up to face the constable.

"For Christ's sake, I didn't ask for a roll-call constable! I asked if anyone was able to identify the deceased! And….excuse me reverend."

A rare apology for McCloud, who then looked to Donahue to continue, if he could.

"Mrs. Johnson believes the deceased is one Alexander Miller, son of MP John Miller, the former banker. Mrs. Johnson wasn't definite, so we've sent a man over to the Miller residence to inquire of Mr. Alexander Miller or find someone to identify him."

The inspector sucked at his teeth, a habit that revealed itself during high stress moments of the job.

He'd begun to look like a man who'd just taken on the weight of a city.

Lost in his thoughts, McCloud slowly paced around the body looking now and then at the face, scrutinizing the features but with no recognition. He knew the Miller family but couldn't recall the last time he had seen the son.

Remembering the minister, he snapped up his head and let out a large and woeful breath.

"You were a witness?" the inspector suddenly inquired. The surprised minister stammered out an answer…

"Yes sir, I was meeting with the parish…"

"Yes, yes, the parish planning committee. Did the deceased say anything before he killed himself? Did he indicate any reason for his distress?"

McCloud fired these questions barely allowing room for a response.

"No sir. Well, he did but…the thing is it wasn't in any kind of language I understood."

"Like what?"

"The only thing I could…well, barely make out…he said something like, … adi-ma-la-ho or… adino malickoy, but, as you can tell, the echo in here makes it difficult to hear specifically what a person says and especially if they have their back to you as the…dead…deceased did… to me."

"Sounds like might've been Hebrew. Anything else?"

"Well, yes. When he said that, he'd raised his arms over his head and made the shape of a triangle with his fingers."

McCloud's eyes flickered with interest at the minister's account and pinching his lips with his thumb and forefinger, answering the minister with a nonchalant, "Hmn…," Another lengthy silence followed, only disturbed when another constable bolted through the front doorway. Sweaty and breathing hard he quickly made his way to McCloud with what was clearly some kind of urgent news.

"Well, spit it out man!"

The constable had stopped dead and was trying to catch his breath.

"Well?"

"A murder sir, in the Ward, a young prostitute it looks like."

"Take down some names and get the particulars. I'll get to it." McCloud waved his hand in dismissal, but the constable refused to move.

McCloud turned those gleaming, cruel eyes to him.

"The thing is, sir, well, she's been cut open, and… parts taken."

"Hell's bells – sorry, reverend - well I can't get there right now.

"Sir, with all respect, rumor on the street has caught like wildfire. Some think Jack the Ripper has come to Toronto."

"Bugger!"

This time, there was no apology to the minister, McCloud was too far-gone in his frustration to excuse himself and had to think quickly. He was short staffed due to the on-going heatwave and its effects, and he definitely didn't want to hand it to another division. This was his beat. There'd also been a stubborn lack of promotions to inspector by the top brass that had plagued his division for a year.

If this was Alexander Miller lying behind him, there was no way he could leave the body. He and the boy's father, John Miller, were old acquaintances. It would have to be him that gave Miller the horrible news. On the other hand, if it wasn't and he didn't get to the Ward to quell the absurd rumor of the Ripper's coming here, the city's press and fear-mongers would have a field day. The fair citizens would panic.

"What about inspector Davies, sir?" Donahue had blurted out without thinking, seeing McCloud was in a bind. Looking back, Donahue would say about this possible career ending moment, *"it was the logical choice."*

McCloud's head snapped up at the mention of Davies' name, his black eyes flashing and seeming full of malice to the young constable.

What Donahue interpreted as mere malice in McCloud was in fact, a deep disdain.

He and Davies had started out as constables together, some 30 years previous. In those days the Toronto force was more like a parish watch.

McCloud, thought of himself as a policeman's policeman, unlike Davies' phony, *man of the people* persona. He knew him for the ex-gang member and thief he was. He never understood the job like McCloud did, always wanting to be everyone's friend, the kid from the Ward made good. He treated the riffraff of the Ward like family, as if he were some kind of savior or working-class hero.

The thought of Davies' esteem from people only fueled his rage and bitter rivalry. He'd far too often been bested by Davies and was loathe to think he envied the man, so, buried the thought. It was far more pleasing to him to think that Davies had had a fall from grace these last few years. Those of the top brass who still supported him were now growing weary of his uncontrolled *habits*.

*What if I do it?* McCloud wondered, spinning a thought over in his mind excitedly. *The Ripper in Toronto?* The idea is growing and McCloud starting to see its possibilities. *This could end Davies.*

"He's still on desk duty, isn't he?" McCloud finally said.

"No sir, he's been on medical leave for the past week."

"Medical leave? Is that what they're calling a weeklong bender nowadays?" McCloud scoffed, a new thought coming to him. *In his condition, Davies was sure to fumble the investigation. When it all falls apart, I'll be there, ready to step in.*

The minister shuffled uncomfortably and trying not to eavesdrop, looked away unable to hide his distaste at what the inspector had said.

Sensing the minister's discomfort, McCloud quickly covered, "not to worry reverend, just a little joke between colleagues," and flashed a disingenuous smile for the benefit of the room. His thoughts though continued to absorb him. *How to do it? Careful now, remember, he knows things about the past, about me. Wait for an opportunity to present itself.*

Donahue forced out a smile in the awkwardness and nodded in turn to the inspector and minister. He hadn't intended on making things difficult but had a habit of speaking before the thought. Then true to form, he jumped in and continued.

"You're obviously in a bind, sir, and, as I remember, inspector Davies does not live far from here. I could get him up to speed and to the murder scene in the Ward, which, as you're aware, he knows well."

McCloud looked at Donahue with his doe eyes, impatient to be thrown a bone. Sure, he'd throw one out, let him fetch Davies.

Looking back at the body McCloud took a moment. Just the right amount of hesitation to seem as though he was thinking over the constable's proposal in depth. In truth, it suited McCloud well.

"Fine. Take your bicycle and get Davies."

McCloud then leaned into Donahue and lowering his voice said, "whatever condition he's in, get him to the Ward. And make sure he reports back to me afterwards."

"Yes, sir."

Donahue, already making his way to the church exit at a sprint, was smiling as if he'd hit the numbers.

Shaking his head, in disbelief of what he'd just set in motion, McCloud spat out the name "Davies" one final time. The church echoed with it as he turned his attention back to the minister.

"So, you were saying he made the sign of a triangle with his fingers…"

CHAPTER 3.

"You better be the devil himself!"

The disembodied voice growled from behind the door of inspector Davies' room as Donahue rapped with equal parts trepidation and urgency.

He had furiously pedaled his constabulary-issue bicycle through the busy noon-hour streets, the stifling heat turning his dark blue uniform heavy and damp with sweat, now the object of his many curses. He'd undone the impressive brass buttons around his collar and, every other minute, needed a sleeve to swipe more sweat away, on this dash to Inspector Davies.

Jimmy Donahue had always dreamed his life as important. That, at any moment, some turn of events, some heroic deed, even a look or a smile, would transport him into the life he wanted for himself, a life beyond the ordinary and mundane.

*This is it! I've finally got a chance to do something.*

*But why did I mention Davies? He* thought, *It just came out.* He knew McCloud was very unsure of his inspector colleague, to say the least. But Davies had also been a hero to lads like himself who'd grown up in the Ward. If Davies could get out, so could they.

*Growing up in the city's core, like he had, you'd be hard-pressed not to know the name Ifan Davies, the first of the wayward inhabitants to make the climb from delinquent to copper. Not a popular choice of profession coming out of the Ward. You'd be held in suspicion by both the police and those still obliged to live there.* Donahue thought, a truth he continued to be confronted with.

Other than the initial response to his knock at the door, no other sound had come from the room. Donahue knocked again.

"Sir, I'm sorry, it's constable James... ah, constable Jimmy Donahue."

He was feeling the full weight of the anticipation that came with this chance to meet the inspector, but his expectations were slowly being diminished by the grim surroundings. Surely an inspector of Davies caliber would be far better off, not living in squalor.

Looking back over his shoulder down the hallway of the rooming house to where he'd come in, he couldn't help feeling sad. The hallway's long-yellowed wallpaper peeling at its edges. Bits of ceiling littered the floor and tattered hall carpeting that was badly stained and smelled of piss. Rat shit here and there. And, from behind some wall down the hall, the sounds of lives that were violent and unrestrained.

A woman and a man were screaming at one another, a turmoil punctuated by the intermittent crash of breaking glass.

*Attempted murder?* Donahue wondered, rubbing his forehead in hope of finding some relief from a headache building behind his temples. As the screaming intensified, he felt torn between his duty and his... duty.

*Was it the inspector who had growled at him? Was the inspector dead? Was he even in the right place? Should I do something about the domestic brawl or press on?*

"I'll kill you; you bitch whore!" Screamed a male voice from down the hall.

Suddenly finding resolve, Donahue made a move toward the ruckus. Yes, Davies would be needed but, yes, there was a potential tragedy at hand, it had also begun to sound as if he, himself, might be witness to the city's next murder.

Just as suddenly, there were the sounds of laughter, tenderness, a cooing couple making up. He shook his head in thankful relief and turned back to his door. It had been opened slightly.

*A strange invitation*, he thought, stepping forward to listen. Not hearing anything he tentatively queried.

"Inspector? Sir?"

Again, there was no response, and he gently poked the door wide enough for a look inside. Nothing was moving, just a dark room with the slightest wisp of light coming through a tattered curtain.

Hearing a rustle from the shadowy outline of a bed, he checked his breath, cheeks flushing as if he'd been caught trespassing, forgetting he'd been invited in. Heart pounding, he swallowed trying to lubricate his parched throat, licking his lips to squeak out a sound he hoped would be a sentence.

The room, stale and humid, smelling of booze and old farts, made him wish he hadn't been so clever suggesting the services of inspector Davies.

"Sir? Hello? Sir?" Donahue managed to get out.

He stepped past the doorway, wondering as he did so, why was he tiptoeing like a scared schoolboy in an abandoned haunted house? *I'm a grown man, here on official police business for Christ's sake*!

"Why are you here, son?" The lumpy shadow on the bed spoke.

A few steps farther and Donahue started making out details. And the first thing that struck him was how small, and pathetic the man that lay before him was, not so much a legend. In the gloom, his idol seemed far too human, and he began to wish he was in the wrong room. He had that sinking feeling that those you've looked up to are not what you hoped.

"My name is Jimmy. Constable Donahue sir…"

"I know your name son, *why* are you here?"

"I was sent by inspector McCloud to fetch you, sir."

The lump exhaled a deep sigh that filled the room, then fell silent again, leaving Donahue to wonder what to do.

It hadn't been until he heard the name McCloud that Davies felt anything resembling life, a life, long marred by one man's conflict with another.

"Fetch? Like a dog? What the hell does that bastard want?"

"Well sir, there has been an incident. Actually, to be precise, there've been a few incidents."

"Constable, I may kill you so, please, do be precise."

"Sir?"

"Brevity I beg you, brevity."

"I see, sir."

"Do you?"

"No, sir."

Flinging aside the shirt he'd wrapped around his head, Ifan grunted and pulled himself up on an elbow and, with his free hand searched the seat of a bare wooden chair he used for a night table. Finding the pre-rolled cigarette he'd placed there in the early morning hours, he put it between his lips and struck a match. The flame illuminated his puffy and splotchy face for a moment and, squinting from the spark he inhaled. He then hacked out the day's first smoke.

Davies's condition took Donahue by surprise, he didn't know what he had expected but quickly looked down at his shoes, hiding his embarrassment.

The few shards of light cutting through the curtains sliced at Ifan's eyes irritating him for a moment. He ducked his head, re-seeking the darkness so he could try and focus on what this young constable was saying, not the pain caused by the light.

"What- do - you - want, constable?"

Ifan had spoken in a controlled and measured manner, barely hiding his irritation, that further unnerved the constable. Donahue hesitated. Davies continued to press.

"If you've taken the trouble to *fetch* me, whatever it is you've come about must be choice. SPEAK, SON!"

"Murder, sir!" Donahue snapped back, then calmed down. "There has been a murder… actually a murder and a suicide."

Donahue, shaking with agitation, stared at Davies not breaking his gaze.

A grin formed at the corner of Ifan's mouth; his eyes beginning to sparkle with a mercurial life. He took a long drag from his cigarette and a barely audible laugh, full of self-knowledge started his body to shaking beyond his control, as he looked sideways at the defiant young constable.

"Very well then. Forgive my appearance constable, you find me not at my best this morning." said Davies, his tone softening, in part acknowledgement of
Donahue's gumption.

"Where you from, son?" Davies continued after a
moment.

"Here, Toronto.

"Where in Toronto?"

Davies was searching Donahue's face the way
one would a person they thought they knew.

"The Ward, sir."

"I see. Good."

At that, Davies jumped up with an alacrity that
surprised Donahue, the man looked dreadful a minute
ago. And not another minute later, Davies was hustling
the young constable out the door while still dressing.

*

On leaving his digs, the inspector had disappeared down an adjacent alley, Donahue close behind,
registering his objections and urging that the inspector
come with him to find a taxi.

"You came by bicycle, I assume."

"Yes, sir."

"Well, then we need to find one for me."

"Excuse, me sir?"

"Appropriating."

Davies began to bubble with excitement, eyes darting left and right as he hurried down the alley checking walkways and back porches. At the far end, stood a simple shack of wood and tarpaper and tucked next to an outhouse, Ifan's ride.

"Ah, opportunity meets need."

"Sir, respectfully, it's theft."

Donahue had whispered for fear of being heard.

"Appropriation for police business. We'll send a thank-you note," said Davies who, without a sound, had deftly grabbed the bike, ran to pick up speed, put a foot to a pedal and, in one swift motion, kicked a leg over the saddle and whisked past the constable.

"Sir!"

Looking back to ensure they hadn't been seen, Donahue then sprinted in the direction of the disappearing inspector.

Donahue had heard the many stories of the one-time thief named Ifan Davies. The police could never pin a thing on him. He was always two steps ahead and, while in the Ward, well-protected from prying eyes.

Myth had it that Davies had been on the streets of the Ward since the age of five, when his mother was said to have died of consumption on the poor house doorstep.

Myth or no, it was true the young Davies had grown up fast and tough and, by the time he was sixteen, was running liquor for one of the old Jewish women bootleggers on Elizabeth Street to the various questionable hotels that dealt in cheap alcohol and prostitution.

By the time he was eighteen, he was running his own gang, thieving, offering protection to various establishments and pimping out a few of the local girls for the swells that liked to slum it on the weekends, feeling like they were down in the nitty-gritty. That would be until Davies and his boys rolled them for whatever cash they had left over, right at the boundary of the Ward and their lives of respectability.

By Ifan's twentieth year, his story becomes a little vague. He was rumored to have shacked up with a young prostitute in a one-room flat somewhere east of Terauley around Edwards. His association with his gang and business partners had slowly begun to disintegrate. Heated words between Davies and gang members ended up in brawls and even a stabbing. There was also the incident that would change the trajectory of Ifan Davies' life forever. The death of his only love.

CHAPTER 4.

John Miller stepped from his carriage, mechanically donning his fine top hat as protection from the relentless sun. Adjusting his vest and smoothing the front of his frock coat, he crossed Bond Street and, under the gaze of a curious press and public, self-consciously began making his way along the footpath to the Metropolitan Methodist.

For most of the last hour or so, he'd been working on convincing himself this was simply a matter of mistaken identity. *This can't be true. No, not my Alexander*, his thoughts trailing off as he noted McCloud waiting for him on the church steps.

"John."

McCloud spoke with a forced business-like calm, not catching Miller's eyes.

Miller reached out his hand, aware the city would soon know how he greeted tragedy.

"William."

Yes, they were old friends but even this simple exchange seemed strained, even cold. Neither could look the other in the eye. Neither knew what to say next. Feeling the whole event some strange and surreal ceremony, McCloud finally took a deep breath and...

"Shall we go in?"

"Thank you, William."

Miller reached for the door but had trouble with its weight and McCloud stepped in to help, ushering Miller into the foyer.

The church was utterly silent. All witnesses to the grizzly event had been questioned and let go

As his eyes adapted to the dimness, Miller could only see a constable from his waist up, the pews blocking any view of what lay at his feet. He moved towards the aisle, stopping at the back row of seating when gripped by a sudden rush of fear.

Sensing an impatience in McCloud, who followed behind, Miller resumed his long and dreaded walk, stopping again, with a shuddering breath, when he arrived at the foot of the chancel.

Alarmed at seeing a father's distress, the constable made an intuitive step forward, but checked himself at the inspector's halting glare.

"Constable, be so kind as to show Mr. Miller the…the unfortunate…"

McCloud found himself at a loss for words to describe the deceased as either victim or suicide, so the word "unfortunate" had hung in the air as Miller, in a daze, looked up to view the expanse of his surroundings.

Hearing but not hearing McCloud and the constable exchange a few words, Miller stood there hoping it wasn't his son.

"If I don't look…" He whispered to himself.

The man was immovable.

Recognizing this, McCloud stepped in behind Miller, gently placed a hand on his shoulder and gave a slight squeeze of encouragement. And, so as not to embarrass him in front of the constable, whispered:

"Are you okay to do this, John?"

"I'm fine, William. Thank you."

At that, Miller stepped forward, eyes fixed on the body that had been covered. The constable, feeling the solemnity of the moment, stepped back to give him room. Stopping just short of the body. Miller looked up to the officer with misting eyes - that he tried to cover, now causing his nose to run. He drew a handkerchief, wiping his nose and upper lip, where a substantially bushy moustache was rapidly turning grey.

"Do you mind, son?"

Miller motioned towards the part of the make-shift shroud that covered the head. The constable knelt, took a corner in hand and, with a slight moment of hesitation, looked up to Miller.

"Sir?"

"Yes."

The cover peeled back, revealing a bruised and swollen face, the right side of it obscured by matted hair blackened with congealed blood.

At first sight, Miller was almost relieved in his horror that the face was unrecognizable, that he was unable to distinguish the features he was sure he knew so well. Slowly, he examined the lifeless face, and began to see. Visions of childhood, laughter, joy, hope, and great expectations appeared and, in the same moment, an overwhelming sense of loss and the deep void of living without shook him to his core.

"Oh God."

As the wilting father buckled at the knees, McCloud and the constable rushed to ease his crumbling to the ground.

CHAPTER 5.

Donahue rode like a man possessed. He'd taken far too long to rouse Davies, ever conscious the situation in the Ward was pressing. Racing west along Queen, he checked over his shoulder periodically to assure the inspector was still following. He was, but badly struggling, wheezing, and sputtering and in obvious discomfort. Neither the heat nor hangover were helping.

The sweat that dripped into Davies' eyes was perfusing and stinging. He was pedaling like hell to keep up with Donahue, and it looked like his ass felt the smart of each bump along the way. They were both struggling to breathe in a humidity that offered no oxygen.

Donahue smiled his amusement, enjoying the spectacle. *Served him right*, he thought, *for stealing the bike.*

The clock tower chimed one as Donahue and Davies passed City Hall. Another block and they'd turn right on Elizabeth, the Ward's main north-south thoroughfare.

St. John's Ward, technically Municipal Ward 3, had a reputation for urban squalor synonymous with immigrant culture and poverty that earned it the derogatory if not dismissive label, The Ward.

As Davies and Donahue cycled up Elizabeth, the street was awash with human traffic. Life made its way onto the streets during the stifling heat of summer, when confined and overcrowded living quarters were rendered unlivable during the day. It was the kind of life that raised anxiety levels for conservative Presbyterian Toronto.

Whenever Ifan crossed the boundary into The Ward, there was always a change in him, both physically and emotionally. Not only was he stepping back in time, but he'd experience an acute sense of time lost. This would make him melancholy and sometimes, paradoxically, irritable to the point of rudeness.

The street was alive with its particular sights, sounds and smells, the comings, and goings of its residents. Hawkers, rag-pickers, derelicts. Men standing in small groups smoking, heads together and talking in tones that implied whatever they were discussing was of the utmost importance or illegal, probably both. Women sitting on their stoops shucking peas into enameled bowels; others sweeping the dust of the city back onto itself.

The old vendors of roasted peanuts and chestnuts, their whistles wafting the smell of their wares, a joy to the many street urchins cajoling for a treat. Fruit sellers pushing their carts north towards College Street, hauling hopes of a new and better life that would begin long after they had walked hundreds of miles and laughed off thousands of slurs, dying before knowing any of the comforts they would pass to the generations to come.

For Ifan, these sights and sounds were a part of his soul, the balm, and dreams of a wayward son.

Even on a day like this, when he was shattered-hungover and shaky, as usual, but also exhausted from his ride through the heat. And on his way to a murder scene.

Two blocks more, through streets swarming with life, they reached Louisa, where some twenty yards to the left, a small crowd gathered at the mouth of a lane-way that was blocked by a few uniforms.

*

It was now close to two hours since the alarm had been raised about the murder.

Donahue wheeled around the corner of Louisa and headed for the crowd of onlookers at the mouth of an alley. His arrival drew scant interest from the assortment of reporters who were sheltering from the sun under shop awnings and vendor umbrellas. A few were taking notes from passers-by; most were simply waiting for something to rouse them from the monotony of waiting when Davies came into view.

Donahue had glided to a stop at the alley where a fellow officer had been melting in the sun.

"Heya Gordie, all under control here?"

"Ya Jimmy. That inspector Davies?"

The two looked back to where Davies had finally decided to abandon his ride, leaning it up against a wall. He'd had a little trouble attempting to dismount.

Coughing and puffing, he was a mess, his dripping face both pale and bloodshot.

Immediately, he was swarmed by the newspaper men shouting over one another, vying for attention.

"Inspector, do you have any leads?"

"Is this some kind of white slavery ring?"

"Have you identified the deceased?"

Davies gave the wheel of his bike one final kick, then muttered something in Welsh, a habit he had when frustrated so he could swear with impunity.

He had always cultivated a jovial relationship with the press, though. Realizing their value and influence with the general public. They were always useful, something McCloud never understood.

"Boys, I just got here. How would I know what's going on?"

"Word on the street says it's the Ripper."

"Well, I guess the case is closed then. I knew City Hall was overpaying me when they could've just asked you boys. I guess we can all go home."

Davies left them laughing as he made his way into the alley. Some twenty yards in, Donahue and his colleague were sharing a smoke over what looked like a rumpled pile of canvas. Seeing the inspector coming, they both ditched their cigarettes like guilty schoolboys caught in the playground.

His senses livening with every step, Davies could feel his heartbeat in his eardrums. His nose began to run, activating a heightened sense of smell.

Outhouses and raw sewage bombarded him, and he felt a rising nausea.

"Cachu" *(Welsh for shit)

"What's that, sir?"

"Welsh."

Donahue eyed the inspector with a worried glance, he did not look forward to the prospect of explaining this to McCloud.

Davies stood a foot from the body, head bowed, hands in his pockets, contemplating the shape and reason for this mess in front of him. The three stood silently for a moment.

"What do you think lads, should we take a look? The two of you lift up the tarp… carefully. Try not to disturb anything that hasn't already been disturbed."

Ifan tilted his head and surveyed the lifeless body. His eyes teared at the sight. He was always emotional at a scene like this. He was never able to develop the cold, detached professionalism of his colleagues.

It was always personal.

What was once a young woman lay half-naked on her back amongst the filth and shit of the alleyway. Her throat had been slit and there was a dark gaping hole, that had been her stomach. Ifan drew in a deep breath and exhaled loudly, the constables moving in for instructions.

"Check in on the alley's houses for anyone who might have seen or heard anything." Davies ordered, wanting some time alone with the victim away from their expectant eyes.

He bent to sit over his heels and began with simple observations, the obvious trauma to the body. The throat had been cut, left to right. A Righthanded person probably, and she'd been attacked from behind. Internal organs had been removed.

He examined the hands, front and back and noticed ligature marks around both wrists. He then took out his pen knife to look under the fingernails. She had all her teeth and very little decay. For a prostitute, she was in very good physical health. Her tattered and bloody clothing was ill-fitting, seeming too small for her frame. The shoes, by contrast, were of good quality, the soles barely worn.

Davies picked up the shoe that lay closest to him, running a hand over the fine silk and embroidered stitching of wildflowers on a background of green. He could still make out the stamped signature of its maker, Angelo di Milano - Italian made. Placing the shoe back in its resting place nearby, he looked over his right shoulder at the plain wood siding of one of the Ward's countless decrepit back-alley shacks and would be homes. These were illegally attached to the fronting buildings, usually right next to the outhouse and raw sewage. Unscrupulous landlords would rent them out, usually five or six to a room.

Slowly rising, Ifan felt the years of wear on his body, the sounds of aching joints and muscles straining to lift him. He reached for his handkerchief, wiped his forehead then the leather band on the inside of his black bowler, cursing his choice over a lighter straw hat.

Damn, it was hot. Was it just his hangover playing havoc?

Scanning the length of the alley, he gave a cursory glance from house to house, not knowing what he was looking for. Something glittering beneath the slatted boards of a makeshift fence a few houses down from the body caught his eye.

He went and picked up a button of highly polished brass from a man's jacket. At its center, an embossed triangle.

From behind the fence, that's when he heard the sound of a heavy, wet cough, followed by some violent spitting up and moans of distress.

Davies went to peer over the fence to see a young Chinese woman, probably in her mid-twenties, laid out on a bed under a large umbrella imprinted with the words Made in Canada. There was also a girl of about seven or eight, gently applying a compress to the woman's forehead. Mother and daughter, he rightly presumed.

"Sorry to disturb, my dear, but does your mother speak English?"

The girl jumped at the sound of the foreign voice but, when she saw the man's soft hazel eyes, sweaty face and funny round hat, her alarm was quickly replaced by a shy amusement. She nodded yes, forgetting for a moment to cool her mother's brow, which elicited a reproachful moan from the woman. She then bent over to whisper something in her mother's ear which caused the woman to look with fear in the direction of the fence then convulse into a violent fit of coughing.

"Sorry madam, I truly don't wish to disturb. My name is inspector Ifan

Davies. Would it be possible to come in and ask a few questions?"

With a weak nod of her head, she motioned the girl to let him in.

Unlatching the gate proved a considerable struggle for her but it eventually scraped open, and the inspector and little girl locked eyes for a moment. She remained both curious and cautious and, in this little person, Ifan could see the concerns and sense of inevitability she lived with. This was probably not the first serious illness the child had dealt with it seemed to Davies.

Going up to the bed, he removed his hat and ducked his head under the umbrella. A thin sheet covered the woman's damp body, clinging to her even though she shook from chills. Her fine black hair was matted and stuck to her face. He turned to the girl:

"TB?"

"The sumption."

"And what's your name?"

"Li Jing," she said, moving back to her place beside her mother. Wringing out the compress in a chipped enamel bowl, then re-applying it, caused the woman's red-rimmed eyes to flutter open briefly.

As the ritual played out, Ifan pulled over an old soapbox crate to sit on, gave his forehead a wipe and, in his most calm and soothing tone:

"As I said, madam, I'm an inspector with the metropolitan police. I was wondering if you might have seen or heard anything last night, since I'm assuming you were most likely sleeping out here."

It was quite possible she'd heard something, but she was obviously suffering with her condition. She blinked then swallowed, trying to form a reply, but ended up shaking her head in an obvious wish the inspector would just leave her be.

"I know it's difficult to speak but, if you could…you see, a young woman was killed just steps from your gate and, if you did hear or see anything, it could be a great help."

Ifan fought off his growing anxiousness as he watched the poor woman try to rally herself to say something, anything. Finally…

"I heard…someone…them… I think, trying to find a way out of the alleyway. They pulled at the gate and woke me."

This burst of speech was followed by another violent coughing fit, her eyes watering as she grasped at her chest wincing in pain. After the storm subsided, Ifan leaned in again.

"Them?" Davies, twigged.

"I heard two, maybe three men."

"Do you remember anything distinct about them?"

"I couldn't see, only shadows behind the gate. I began to cough, and they ran off."

"Did you recognize any of the voices, as from the neighborhood?"

"No."

"Does anything else come to mind? Please, anything at all?"

The girl leaned into her mother and whispered something into her ear. The woman nodded, drew a deep breath, then focused hard into the eyes of the inspector.

"One of them…"

"Yes?"

"One was giving orders to the others. He spoke fancy. Not from the neighborhood."

"British?"

"No, fake…swanky."

Looking blankly at Ifan, she gave into another bout of wet coughing, the girl readying a nearby bucket. Ifan stood to go.

"Thank you for…"

He didn't finish the sentence. Looking at the two, he knew their outcome as well as they did. There was no acknowledgment of his leaving. What was the point when there is dying to do.

*

The constables were already standing by the body when Davies returned.

"And what is it you two have found?"

"Some writing, sir."

"Writing?"

"Graffiti, sir. Near the entrance to the alley."

Davies briskly headed off, the constables scampering to keep up. The graffiti would be one thing, but he also wanted to scan the onlookers in the street, specifically for the reporters. He was only a few feet from the crowd when the constables caught up.

"Sir? Over this way."

"What's that?"

"The graffiti."

"What's it says?"

Donahue was confused. The graffiti was right there on the wall, a few feet away. The inspector could easily see for himself. Instead, trying not to be overheard by the crowd, Donahue read the writing aloud.

"What was that constable?"

Davies, again looking in the wrong direction, had turned towards Donahue, pointed at his ear as if to say, he was bit deaf.

Frustration setting in, as well as another reminder that his suggestion Davies be brought on board might've been a terrible mistake, Donahue, without fully thinking, yelled out:

"The Jews are the men that will not be blamed for nothing"

"And how is Jews spelled?"

Surprised by Davies' sudden canny, intuitiveness, Donahue could only comply:

"J-U-E-W-S."

Out of the corner of his eye, Davies noted one of the reporters twig to this, then stare in disbelief at his colleagues. The newspapermen suddenly ran off in every direction and the crowd began to buzz. Davies overheard someone say, "it is the Ripper;" another, "Jack the Ripper? Here?"

Poor Donahue looked around at the excited crowd, not exactly sure what had just happened. He cast a desperate look towards the inspector.

"Oh, damn," he mumbled as Davies moved past him to focus on the graffiti.

Written in chalk were the exact words that had been left behind in England's White Chapel murders some eleven years previous.

He continued staring at the words, while a faint smirk starting to show at the corner of his mouth.

"Mmn hmmn."

Davies turned swiftly to face whom ever had cleared their throat behind him, expecting Donahue, he was surprised to find a lone newsman grinning at him.

"Aren't you gonna run off and file your sensational story like the rest of them, Joe?" Davies said, flicking his head toward the street.

"Ifan Davies, as I live and breathe, haven't seen you on the beat in a long while."

"Joe Levy, you still working for that rag of yellow journalism they call the Star?"

"Yup, still on the crime beat, as you can see. I take umbrage you call it a rag though. We're the only paper that cares about the interests of the ordinary people."

"Shit Joe, you sound like the advertisers."

The two shared a laugh and shook hands, both keeping a sideways watch on the other. Levy offered a cigarette and the two smoked in silence watching the scene before them.

Donahue was overseeing those who had just arrived to load the body onto the morgue wagon, while a few other officers dispersed the remaining crowd.

Levy, a savvy, street smart reporter of about the same age as Davies, yet far stouter, was content for the moment to wait out Davies' silence. Just smoke. He knew Davies was mulling over what he could, would, tell him and, what he was going to keep to himself.

Levy was starting to get the itch to ask some questions and was thinking, Davies is taking his time with that smoke. "Good to see ya back workin." He offered up finally, not looking at Davies.

"Had to take some time off."

"Time off, huh. That's what you're calling it?"

"You probably want to know what I'm thinking."

"Yup."

"Just print it's the Ripper."

Levy nodded; Davies flicked his butt in return and the two parted.

*Now, let the press do its work*, thought Davies.

CHAPTER 6.

Shadows were stretching long and hot across Louisa Street as Ifan finally stepped out of the alley. The reporters had long ago scattered, and the crowd lost interest once the cart from the morgue had been loaded and pulled away into a low hanging sun.

He dug out his well-worn tobacco tin, plucked his last pre-rolled from amidst the loose tobacco and rolling papers, lit up and took a long, deep pull. Dropping his head back, he blew a rolling white cloud out into the air.

*Fyyc fe (Fuck it, in Welsh)*, he thought, and started to walk east towards Terauley, then north at the corner. The Ward's sights and sounds enveloped him as he made his way, half in a trance, with no real destination. He'd do that when he was trying to think, just start walking and see where his feet would take him.

Thoughts and memories bounced through his mind, the past mingling with the present, tumbling over one another, even as he kept his gaze straight ahead, all in soft focus.

He soon found himself at Edward, turned east again but, after only a few steps, stopped and slid into the recess of a doorway. He was focused on a small lane that ran north, specifically on a very familiar green door.

Maybe another cigarette. He'd have to roll one, though, a bit of a trick given how badly his hands were shaking. His eyes fixed on that entranceway; he began pulling at the fixings in his tin.

He stood looking back in time. Nothing had changed, but he had, the rest of the world had. Life moved all around him, no past, no present, no future. Tears began to mist his eyes and he could feel his heart shatter into pieces. Again. *Why had his feet taken him here?* Apparently, they had a mind of their own.

Her name was Hèlene, a young woman with the bluest eyes he'd ever seen. They had pierced his heart the day he looked up and fell into them.

She could make a sailor blush, as they say, expressing herself freely in a world of confined rules for women. Ifan admired that in her. Unlike himself, she never seemed self-conscious or ill at ease, never showed any fear of the world. With head high and eyes ablaze, she confronted every hardship that life threw at her and, as a working girl, those were many.

He was so smitten, so fearful of even speaking to her, he needed best friend Mickey Doolan to work out an introduction. When that happened, he spoke, and she spoke, and they found out they enjoyed talking to one another.

So far gone into this time gone by, Davies never heard his name being called from across the street.

"Ifan! Ifan! Hey, you, silly copper. What the hell you staring at and looking like a damn fool? Oh, you are a sad sight. Yes, up here!"

Crawling out from under his memories, he lifted his head to see the glorious vision of Mama, a large woman of uncertain origin and wealth who loved to smoke cigars and dress like a gypsy in bright silk head scarfs and gold hoop earrings. She was leaning out of a second-storey window, waving at him to come closer.

"Oof! You were always a pitiful boy!"

"And you were always a hard ass, Mama."

"Damn right. Let you boys take an inch…"

"You just gonna yell at me in the streets or let me up?"

She reached into her ample bosom, pulling out a set of keys and, with a wide grin and haul on her cigar, dropped them to the ground. Ifan had his bowler ready for the catch, stubbed his smoke and headed upstairs.

No one, not even he, knew Mama's full name or full story. Like his, her story was part real, part myth.

She'd been part of the first wave of Jewish and European immigrants to Canada, the ones that could, and did, assimilate into the British North American culture. Not like these new Eastern European Jews, as was heard from many of those who had already staked a life and territory here. Mama, however, flaunted her difference and invented her exoticism. She wasn't going to be poor and, if the men that came to her were looking for a gypsy woman of mystery, instead of the Jewish girl from around the block, she'd give it to them. And would make them pay for it.

Mama created and developed the character she would become by appropriating bits from the many cultures that made their way through the Ward. The Roma was from Eastern Europe, most obviously, but she also held a fascination with the black community that came to thrive here after escaping slavery. There were also her own mystic Jewish roots and Yiddish language, of course, and to all of this, a generous dash of the theatrical.

Her choices were not always popular with those in her community, but she soon began amassing money and influence, an influence that came with the names of clients with specific tastes and desires.

Making his way up the thin black and white tiled staircase that sloped to the right, Ifan began taking off his jacket and unbuttoning his collar. It became warmer with each step owing to Mama having the, sometimes, good fortune to live directly above a Chinese laundry, where vats boiled water day and night. The steam mixing with the already damp, hot air turned the rooms above into a sweatbox during the summer. The good fortune came in the winter.

Ifan wasn't just shedding his clothes with every step but the persona he carried out in the world. He had taught himself to talk like them, to hold himself like them. He had co-opted and mimicked to get along.

Now, he could feel his body changing, so that it was no longer detached from his true self. He would speak differently, walk differently. Yes, he was home.

He put a key to the familiar door with the chipped red paint, opening it into a bright world of peacock feathers, Chinese paper lanterns, beaded doorways, worn Persian rugs and vividly coloured satin pillows. A dream-like haze smelled of cigars, laundry steam and the unmistakable odor of sex. From the rooms down the long hallway to the left, came the sounds of grunting, squealing and rhythmic banging.

Mama sat fanning herself at the window to his right, perched on a highbacked chair, throne-like. Yes, that was why he'd often thought of her as queen of all she surveyed.

"Business sounds brisk."

"This an official visit?"

"No."

"In that case, come here and give me some lovin'."

Ifan stepped across the room to become enveloped in Mama's huge, outstretched arms that somehow completed the feeling he was having about being a truant son returning.  Then, holding him at arms-length, she searched his eyes and sweaty face.

"I know it's hot but the sweat that's drippin' from you ain't from the heat. You got the flops, baby."

He broke her gaze, fell silent a moment, handed back the keys, then went for his tobacco tin, pausing when he saw how badly his hand was shaking. He held it out to show her.

"And this…."

"You're making that beautiful face old before its time."

"Just trying to forget."

"There ain't no forgetting, just dying baby," said Mama, trying to catch his gaze.

Ifan slipped into a small wooden chair, dropped his head back, took a deep breath and closed his eyes.

"I'm weary, Mama."

"Why you here?"

"I don't know."

"Okay, you don't know."

"My dissolution with the world is almost complete, Mama."

"Well, aren't you tragic. I thought, of all my boys, you'd have far more gumption. Guess I was wrong." Mama paused, then. "I almost never see you any-more."

But for the sound of that business down the hall, another silence fell between the two. Ifan was struggling with what he was trying to express, every uncomfortable inch of him a boy wanting to confess. Finally, he lit a cigarette, drew deeply, then launched into his thoughts.

"I can't sleep, Mama, I can't eat, I can't do my job. I drink and it blessedly all goes away but at night... oh, at night, the terrors, and memories. Waking up is worse. It all gets...look at my hands! I hide them in my pocket so no one will notice me shaking. I bark and growl...."

His voice broke into a dry rasp, his words falling away as he took another haul on his smoke. He looked up searching for help.

Mama had already turned her attention to a small wooden side table, pulling at its decorative face to pop open a small, secret drawer. It struck him as a strange and delicately winsome act for the size of the woman.

The little brown ball Mama was now rolling between her thumb and forefinger, was pungent in the thick damp air. Ifan unconsciously licked his lips.

"I have something that might help you through the day. I see you know what this is."

"I am an inspector, Mama."

"You've used hashish before?"

"No."

"Well then, a very little of this mixed in your tobacco, you can calm the nerves, steady the hands. A little more at night will help you with the terrors, bring you sleep."

For Mama, knowing her boy's turmoil and sadness, this was the only solace she knew to offer. She placed it in his palm and closed his fist around it, never releasing him from her gaze.

"Use just a little at a time. Too much and you'll be useless. And no booze!"

He studied the hash a moment in his palm, then tucked it among the shag in his tin, an instinctual precaution. He stubbed out his smoke on the heel of his boot, throwing the dog-end out the window as he got up. Then hooking a finger into his jacket, flicked it over his shoulder and searched for something to say. His professional self was coming back.

"Keep your girls close for a while."

"So, you believe it's the Ripper?"

"Who told you that?"

"Word travels fast in the Ward, you know that. So, is it true?"

"I don't know yet… Oh, here's your key."

"Keep it. Maybe you'll visit more often?"

Ifan took a step towards the door, awkward and unfulfilled, then stopped to look back.

"I miss her, Mama."

"I know you do, baby."

It was then he remembered the brass button he'd found in the alley. He dug it out of his pocket and held it out to her.

"I almost forgot. You ever seen a button like this on any of your clients? It's quite unusual. See the raised triangle?"

Mama glanced at it with the bored expression of persons in service that said, *I don't give a damn or care what the punters wear, as long as they pay.*

"No."

CHAPTER 7.

Stepping out into the street, Davies felt he could breathe again. The day had wound down into mid-evening, and he headed west on Edward toward Elizabeth.

The rag dealers and garbage pickers were going through the day's trash, looking to salvage anything of worth. The young didn't go for the rag trade, so it was mostly made up of the dispossessed, the mad and the elderly who kept life and limb together until disease and death relieved them from the drudgery and dismay of existence.

Among a small group working over a pile of refuse, his cart loaded with a mix of cheap trinkets and new-found treasures, was the man they called King Sol.

From Eastern Europe, they say, and now living in the shadows of St. John's Shtetl, a few blocks south.

Ifan had heard the stories that the man never slept or stopped moving, that no one knew where he actually laid his head. To the inspector, this nocturnal who knew everything and everyone that moved through the night in the Ward, had always been his eyes and ears of the quarter.

"King! Over here."

The old man, seventy-five maybe, lifted his tired head towards the voice and squinted through half-closed eyes stinging with sweat. When he made out it was Ifan, he smiled a rotten-tooth smile through a beard of steel-wool and waved.

As he made his way to him, he had to admire the elegance with which Sol pulled a handkerchief from his breast pocket to wipe his hands and present a clean, dry palm in friendship.

*Always the gracious King*, noted Davies, returning the gesture and, as always, surprised at the strength in the old guy's grip. Always the host of the streets.

"Boychick, it has been too long. What, I don't see you no more? Who comes and has a glass tea with me? Nobody, I tell you, nobody."

Ifan looked warmly on the old man but said nothing, making Sol uncomfortable enough that he started picking at the strands of his tallith that poked out from under his dirty waistcoat.

"So, you just going to stand there? Cat caught your tongue or what?"

"No, just looking at you. It's good to see you, old friend."

"Old, hmm, he calls me old. But why not? I am. You buying or just looking?"

With his customary flourish, Sol lifted his hands to the sky then presented his cart for inspection. It was filled with penny amusements, candies in colourful paper, alongside a few household items and old tobacco tins. Ifan plucked a candy from the pile and flipped the King a coin.

"Well, thank you, Mr. Baron.

"Mmm, orange."

"The most popular."

Ifan played with the wrapper, folding it into a small square, then asked…

"Were you out last night, King?"

"I'm always out."

"Were you anywhere near Louisa Street?"

The King scanned the street around him, silently got behind his cart and pushed it into motion. Ifan strode easily behind and the two walked in silence to the end of the block, when Sol spied a fresh pile of trash and rushed ahead.

"Look at this! People today…hmm…just throw away a perfectly good chair.

A little work, good as new."

Catching up to the King, Ifan pressed him:

"What aren't you saying, King?"

Freeing a piece of fabric from the pile, Sol gave it a sniff then pocketed it.

"This is about the poor girl you found, is it?"

"It is."

"I got nothing to say."

"Sol? What are you trying to save me from?"

"Yourself."

"That's not an answer."

The King was silent as he shifted his gaze from Ifan to the pile of garbage, then up then down the street, then back to him. "The one you call the short one..." then with a sigh of resignation, "from Mickey Doolan's gang."

"You mean Little Sean?"

The King nodded, still trying to look busy.

"What about him, King?"

"I see him coming out of that alley last night."

Again, the King was evasive.

"And?"

"I see first, one man, follow him out. I wait a bit, and then, another."

"Did you recognize them, see their faces?"

"No, it was too dark, I only recognize the Sean guy."

"What time was it?"

"I don't know boychick, 3:30 – 4am, maybe."

Ifan was starting to shake with anxiety, his temper getting short along with his patience. When his chest began to pound, he knew withdrawal was kicking in.

It had been the previous night or very early morning since he'd last had a drink

"Okay, I thank you, King, but look, this is important. Think if there was anything about them that might be familiar. Please…"

"I told you, what I told you. Boychick, I ain't got time to talk. I don't bug you at work, huh?" King said pushing past Ifan, determined to fill his cart.

CHAPTER 8.

The evening papers had hit the streets when Donahue got back to the squad-room at Division. The newsies wouldn't have any trouble selling out.

The squad-room was absolutely buzzing. Donahue could see Inspector McCloud pacing his office reading one of the city's broadsheets. Even from twenty yards, he could tell storm clouds were gathering.

He found a desk as far away as possible to get working on his report. He wouldn't risk even a glance towards the office for fear of being noticed then summoned, or worse, assigned some menial tasks.

Donahue wrote swiftly and with such intent that he didn't feel the tap on his back and, indeed, didn't move at all until the strong, firm grip on his shoulder. Annoyed, he swiveled in his chair ready to fling some verbal abuse. Then he saw it was McCloud.

The two locked eyes for a moment, McCloud's contempt palpable, as Donahue feigned composure. McCloud simply jerked his head towards his office, then briskly walked away. Donahue followed, feeling every eye in the room upon him.

McCloud stood with his back to the door, newspaper in hand, all the while fuming. Why he had drawn McCloud's ire remained a mystery to Donahue, but it was obvious he was going to be tortured with silence as long as possible. Finally, McCloud threw the broadsheet onto his desk.

"Please explain to me what the hell this is?"

Looking into the twisted anger of the Inspector's face, Donahue wished he had said: "It's a newspaper, you asshole. What do you think it is!?"

Instead, he opted for…

"Exactly what do you mean sir?"

"I mean this, here!"

McCloud was stabbing his finger at the paper, specifically at the huge, bold headline splashed across the top of the front page: RIPPER COMES TO TO-RONTO. Donahue bent slightly over the Inspector's desk to get a better view.

"Yes?"

"What do you mean, 'yes?' Yes, you knew about it? Yes, you were the source of this?"

"It's already rampant rumour in the Ward. I don't think I was any source."

"No?"

"I didn't speak to any newspapermen. Nobody spoke to them."

Donahue felt more defiant the more he spoke and, as he stood his ground, the inspector took on a slightly friendlier countenance.

"How was it, then, that newspapermen concluded we're hunting Jack the bloody Ripper? That, after an eleven-year hiatus, he's now here in this city?"

"Well, I guess they might have got some notion when I was relaying some information to the Inspector."

"Information?"

"Yes, sir. Inspector Davies was having some trouble hearing."

"And…?"

"I had to yell to him, sir."

"And what was it you had to yell to him?"

"Nothing about…well, it was just some things we had found. Some graffiti and such."

"And what did this graffiti say, if you don't mind me asking?"

Donahue pulled out his notebook, flipped to the spot, turned the page towards the inspector and read:

"'The Jews are the men that will not be blamed for nothing.' The Inspector was also interested, in particular, how Jews was spelled, and that was j-u-e-w-s." McCloud said under his breath, and closing his eyes, rubbed his forehead, and exhaled heavily. A slight smile began to form, followed by an almost imperceptible self-conscious laugh.

"And where is Davies now?"

"Sorry, sir, I don't know. I thought he'd be here."
The storm clouds were forming again.

"Find that f…bring me Davies, right now!"

"I have no idea where he is, sir."

"Well, you'd better find him, boyo, or this is your
last day in the uniform of the Metropolitan Constabulary. Do you hear me?"

McCloud was now livid. It wasn't so much the
newspapers, but the sinking feeling that Davies was
cooking up something, and that he wouldn't be able to
control him. Then there was the innocent and shocked
look on Donahue's face that only fed his anger.

He began to slowly tear his newspaper, and with
a calm expression, locked his dead-pan eyes on Donahue.

The young constable backed out into the squad
room a chill running up his spine watching this controlled malice.

And, with a final "Find Davies or you're done,"
McCloud slammed his door.

Donahue's mind was spinning as he got back to
his desk.

*Where would Davies go? Home? What home? I
thought he would be here. Why isn't he here? What*

*was that all about? Nobody said a word to the press. The inspector's an asshole. God, I'm starving. I haven't had a bite all day. I've got to take a piss.*

He went back to his notebook. Staring down at the page, his heart starting to race with an unsettling realization. *The graffiti! God! It's the very same message left behind at the White Chapel murders.* Donahue was only ten when the details were printed, that misspelling, though…somehow it stuck with him.

Unwittingly, he had told the press Jack the Ripper was alive and well, living in the city. His stomach turned.

CHAPTER 9.

Davies stood across the street from the basement entrance of one of the city's many illegal beer shops or, as they were more lovingly known in the Ward, blind pigs, or blind tigers.

It was well into mid-evening, but the heat persisted, galling his very existence, which hadn't been going very well in any case.

*Maybe a quick drink to take the edge off?* Then he thought he just might shit himself. Then he decided: *No, just get this one thing done.*

He moved toward the non-descript entrance, a door of rusting steel with no markings that suggested any kind of trade or human activity. Suddenly, he stopped short and, ducking up an adjacent alley, doubled over in pain. He slid into a doorway, punched his thigh to distract from the grief in his gut and began mumbling to himself. More truthfully, berating himself for this weakness. "CACHAUBANT!" (Welsh for fuck off) Davies hissed out, clenching his teeth.

He felt his chest constricting and moaned as he clutched at his ribs. A little whimper escaped his tightly held jaw and, somehow, he felt some sense of gratitude for the darkness that offered the quiet favor of obscurity.

*Was it his withdrawal or nerves about the confrontation he knew was ahead?* Bracing himself against the door frame, even that simple question was unclear. Then he remembered the gift from Mama.

He squatted deep in the doorway's shadow to roll up a cigarette, this time breaking off a piece of the hash and crumbling small bits over the tobacco.

Lighting it, he took a long, deep haul and held it.

When he finally exhaled, he also seemed to let go some of the anxiety that had gripped him but, within seconds, was overwhelmed by nausea. He at least managed to get to his hands and knees to spew the contents of his guts which consisted of little more than bile and the booze he had the night before. Tasting bitter, he spit its remnants from his lips.

He turned to sit, wiping his mouth with the back of his hand. He couldn't tell if it was the drug or his withdrawal. But he could tell he was calming, his breathing becoming regular, same for his heartbeat. Next came the beginning of a sense of euphoria.

He got to his feet, moved 'round to the door of the beer shop, took one final moment to collect himself, then reached for the handle.

Mickey Doolan's cruel, scarred face, shaved head and dirty beard was the first thing Davies saw as he stood at the top of the three four steps leading down to the bar. All other heads turned towards the stranger as the heavy door slammed behind him.

"Well, look what the cat dragged in, boys."

Doolan stood up from behind the table where he'd been holding court, a malicious smile breaking across his face as he waved Davies in with a quick gesture of his hand.

Ifan smiled, thinking, *boy Mickey's put on a few pounds.*

"Ifan foockin' Davies, now don't cha have a set of balls on ya to drag your ugly copper carcass inta my fine establishment."

"Mickey."

"Ifan."

With that briefest of greetings, the hive of business and the business of drinking came to a halt, all eyes now swiveling between the two one-time best friends.

The hashish was starting to take effect as Ifan started down the few steps that led into the beer shop, giving the gas-lit room a particular gloom. To him, it always looked more like a root cellar with its dank stone walls and the musty smell of the cobbled floor blending with that of thick tobacco smoke, sweat and a hint of piss.

The dimness allowed for any number of illegal activities and hid the ugly of the world in its corners, out of sight of the law and whatever element of polite society might ever chance by. It offered none of the quaint pleasures of the local taverns, but nor the prices, which made Mickey's place so essential to its people. In truth, it provided simple haven for the hard -working men, women, and poor of the city to drink down the little bit of comfort they could afford.

Doolan, himself, one of the final vestiges of the Ward's old Irish gangs, was beloved by those who grunted out their lives here -- the working poor man's hero. He always had time and a bit of money - or dope - if you needed it. He'd spot you a drink 'til payday. He'd be there to help out your old Ma. And, unlike the intellectual, snooty do-gooders who came to the Ward to "help," he was no phony.

Ifan clocked the room, noting Doolan's men beginning to close ranks, hands in pockets or reaching into hiding spots that concealed the force that maintained the empire. He paused at the last step, smiled at Doolan, then opened his jacket wide for all to see he was unarmed. The whole room resumed breathing.

"Now, what could bring your shitty-arsed face into my establishment?"

Doolan, the ever-gracious host, pointed to an empty chair at his table. Ifan, with another quick look around the room, gingerly took the offer, saying nothing.

Doolan laughed that inaudible laugh that was self-knowledge.

"Lookin' for someone is it?"

Ifan crossed his legs, placed his bowler on his knee and, with the brush of his hand idly wiped a small speck of dirt from the brim. Slowly lifting his head, he locked eyes with Doolan but said nothing.

"Will ya have a drink, boyo?"

Ifan shook his head slowly and continued his unwavering gaze. The chess match between the two was well underway and the more Ifan stared, the more Doolan tried to cover his discomfort. Doolan let out a laugh, rocked back on the legs of his chair and placed his hands in his waistcoat's pockets, assuming nonchalance. Looking around to the men that were eager to pounce for their master, he threw out tidbits for their enjoyment.

"Now ya see, boys, only a stupid copper would come in here and refuse a drink, not like smarter lads over at the Division. But Ifan here was always a bit dim."

Ifan just nodded, smiling to himself at the affect he was having on Doolan.

"Well, as fun as this has been seeing you again, Ifan, I do have business to attend to," said Doolan, clearly nearing the end of his patience. "Now, did ya just come here to look lovingly into my eyes, or ...do you HAVE SOMETHIN' TO FOOCKIN' SAY?"

The room fell silent as Doolan leaned forward over the table and let his spittle fly in Ifan's face. Ifan never flinched, calmly took his handkerchief to wipe away the angry spray, leaned in to go nose- to- nose. And, in the most controlled manner…

"I didn't come to speak to you. I'm looking for Little Sean. You wouldn't happen to know where he is now, would you?"

Ifan could feel the sweat dripping down the back of his neck, a single drop travelling the length of his spine to find the crack of his ass. This wasn't a distraction, but a pleasure. He felt alive with the sweat of both excitement and fear.

"Haven't seen him in days."

"Hmm, that's not what I've heard."

"And what is it you've heard?"

"Well, that would be the opposite of what you just said."

"What?"

"That you haven't seen him in days."

The sweetness of Doolan's voice dripped honey: "And who told you that?"

"No one you would know."

"But I know everyone; they all know me."

"Yes, Mickey Doolan, king of the ward. Nothing happens here that Mickey doesn't know."

"Ya, that's right."

"Then you know that your boy was seen coming out of the alley off Louisa Street last night."

"What of it?"

"Funny thing, but a girl was murdered in that alley last night. And your boy was seen there."

The room was now riveted on the conversation. Mickey Doolan's renowned temper was beginning to seep through the cracks in his veneer, all the while stoked by Davies' unwavering composure. The patrons' excitement was palpable.

"You keep saying my 'boy,' as if I had any control over a grown man."

"Come on, Mickey, don't be so modest. We both know control over another human being is exactly what you do, whether it be prostitution, extortion, gambling…"

"Shut up."

"Cachau – bant." (fuck off).

"Speak English, you Welsh idiot!"

Ifan didn't flinch at Mickey's anger. Acting as stoker to the flame, he said slowly…

"Pen pidyn." (dick head)

With a gruesome yell and reddening face, Doolan slammed his fists into the tabletop, sending drinks to the floor and scattering bystanders. The hashish now in full effect, Davies returned an oddly quizzical look -- as if he were watching a comedy at the theatre.

It was from that from that point on that, Ifan would have trouble remembering the order of events. He had just thought, *Am I really doing this? I feel…* when Doolan's fist hit him smack between the eyes, toppling him backwards off his chair.

Now in some long tunnel, he sensed Doolan's voice: "Nobody touch him, he's mine!" Then there were these massive hands grabbing him by his lapels, pulling him to his feet, and a rain of crushing blows to his face and body. His own hands felt encased in cement and couldn't be lifted. He was being dragged somewhere.

*

There was a sudden rush of fresh air, the sound of laughter and a cascade of warm piss on his face. Mickey Doolan's moist, liquored breath was very close. A whisper in his ear: "You don't belong here. Crawl back into that bottle you came from."

All started turning black but, from deep in the background, through the cheers and yelps from taunting men, a whistle. And, through all that racket, as he began to drift, another voice. He couldn't quite find the memory, but, as a blurry body leaned over to, what? help him? He recognized - or thought he recognized - the frightened face of the young constable Donahue.

CHAPTER 10.

"Hehe he, pen pidyn!" (dick head)

That came from the mostly limp body draped over the saddle as the bicycle hit a pothole.

Donahue was considering himself fortunate that a couple of Chinese gents happened to be passing by the alley, most likely having been at one of the Mahjong parlors in the area, when they heard his whistle. They'd given him a hand getting the, more or less, unconscious inspector precariously balanced over the bike, then wished him luck, and quickly walked away, whispering, and laughing animatedly to one another.

Looking around to see if any other prying eyes would add to the humiliation, the constable gently steered his bicycle toward another pothole, which would soon prompt another moan and more Welsh. Donahue couldn't help the delight that began to spread through him.

Crashing through the door of his bed-sit, Donahue let the inspector hit the floor in a not-to-graceful manner. The thump, wet and heavy, would do nothing to disturb the rest of house. The day-laborers who rented there slept like the dead, rose with the sun, and almost never heard the constable's comings and goings.

Lighting the lamp next to his bed, the spartan room glowed orange, black smoke rose from the fluted lampshade and dispersed its oily smell. He had begun unbuttoning his uniform when Davies let out a moan, rolled onto his back, sputtered, then spit up on himself.

"Ugh, no."

Donahue looked away, then decided the inspector wasn't smelling so good, that he really should give his face a wipe. He found a cloth he'd used that morning, gave it a rinse in what water he had left and, with a few cursory swipes, went beyond the call of duty.

Donahue had also thought of sharing one of his pillows with the inspector but a certain mischievousness in his personality - that Davies, himself, had been stirring in him - won out.

"You twit," he said, tossing the inspector's bowler onto his chest where he lay.

He went back to his routine, meticulously brushing and setting out his uniform for the next day on his poor-man's valet - the only thing his mother had given him when he went to make his way in the world. He checked the collar of his shirt, pulled a freshly starched one from a small chest of drawers, switched them out, then hung the shirt above the doorway for airing out.

He applied the same meticulous eye to his boots, pulling a rag from a shoe box under the bed, spitting on each, then rubbing away the grime of the city. Lining them up next to his side table, he draped his socks over their openings and blew out the lamp.

Donahue lay motionless on top of the sheets, the night too hot for sleep, and looked enviously at the inspector.

*

The last thing Davies remembered, would remember, was the force of Mickey Doolan's fist. It hadn't been so much pain as surprise, the hash dulling his senses and reaction time. The whole episode had been in slow motion and, in his own words - as he somehow recalled while being dropped to Donahue's floor - now seemed foolish.

With the taste of salt and iron in his mouth and a swollen eye refusing to open, he gave over to his wounds. The dope, the heat, the beating he had taken, the euphoric high mixed with adrenaline … all of it started to carry him away. And the dreams and memories that arrived felt as true, as real, as the day they were created.

*

"Inspector? Sir, you have to get up now."

Davies heard Donahue's voice somewhere in the recess of his consciousness, not knowing if he was awake or just about to be awake. Snatching at the few remnants of a dream that had not yet dissolved, he felt overcome with a sense of loss.

But he knew that voice … just couldn't put a face to it, nor why it was here bothering him so early. *And in his room!*

With a start that shakes a person when they realize that they are not where they expect to be, crawling back to reality from a dreamscape, Ifan opened his eyes in confusion. He was hardly less confused when there, standing over, all clean shaven and buttoned up, was that constable Donahue.

"Hope you slept well, sir. I'm to take you to inspector McCloud. He's expecting you."

After a restless, sweaty night, Donahue had got up early, went to fetch water for the jug on his washstand and took a wash and a shave, both quick but refreshing. His shirt was still damp but, with the new collar, he could get away with one more day.

Still puzzled by Donahue's presence Ifan shifted his gaze to take in the room and his position, which he now assessed to be the floor, given the angle he was seeing the officer at and the sharp pain in his neck and lower back.

He closed his eyes, thinking back through the evening, but the vast blankness of it all offered him nothing. Except for the occasional flash of Mickey Doolan's ugly face.

*Oh yeah…now it's clear, well not clear, but I'm pretty sure it's coming back,*

Ifan thought as he opened his eyes again

"Did you have a fine sleep, sir?"

"No. And what's that you're holding?"

"Coffee, sir."

"For me?"

"Sorry, sir, I've just done with it."

"There wouldn't happen to be any more to be had?"

Ifan watched as Donahue drank the last gulp of coffee down. He sensed he should be putting on his best manners, realizing that the constable had somehow got him out of harm's way.

"Sorry, sir. There's only one pot made in the morning by the landlord's wife and, if you're not up to get it, you do without."

Davies winced as he lifted himself to lean up against the bed.

"Fair enough, God, I hurt. Was I run over by a coach and six?"

"No, Mickey Doolan."

"How do you know that? I don't remember you there. I can barely recall me being there."

"I broke it up and got you out of that alley."

Davies looked up at Donahue, then stretched out his hand for the constable to help him up.

"Jesus, I stink. Can I get a quick wash? How about a cigarette first?"

*

Davies could feel the mood in the squad room grow tense as he made his way through division. A step behind, Donahue had whispered "good luck" and went to find a desk with a clear view of the glass partition surrounding McCloud's office, then took to looking busy.

Davies had to pause a moment to consider the strange piece of theatre this seemed – McCloud pacing his office, speaking agitatedly on his phone; the rest of the room, fully aware of the situation, doing its business-as-usual best to ignore it.

He had no doubt that he was an integral part of the drama and, with a grin he couldn't help, knocked at the office door.

McCloud jerked his head violently towards the interruption, prepared to eviscerate the culprit, but, seeing Davies, muttered a few closing words into the phone and waved him in, a malicious smile and deep contempt now clearly part of his countenance.

Davies stepped inside, enjoying the obvious irritation he was causing and, for that first moment or two, he and McCloud stood like gamblers searching for a tell.

He soon realized they were not alone when, out of a shadowy corner that housed a coat rack and tall, wooden filing cabinet, stepped the well-put-together figure of The Right Honourable Franklin Ashfield, Member of Parliament.

"Good morning, Inspector Davies."

Ifan had an instant read on the man, and it started with a discernable hint of arrogance and an impeccably tailored suit. The kind of man for whom, no matter how hot and humid, not a solitary drop of sweat would seep through his immaculate haberdashery. He could stand the whole day in that black suit, in the full sun, and his brow would never dampen.

There is a particular type of suit worn by a particular type of person that no other can carry off. It's not the material, the fine stitching, or the fact that it didn't even have a label. It is the how that person wore it. And only a few could carry it off.

Growing up where he had, Ifan was able to distinguish the difference between those who pretended to have money and those who were born to it. The latter never cared or worried about it for the simple reason they always knew that money, food, and clothing would always be there, not only amply, but superbly, beautifully.

This knowledge was not only comforting, but changed the person from within, how they carried themselves and how the clothes they wore hung off them. They knew they were privileged and loved themselves in their luxury. And, unlike the self-consciousness of those newly rich, the privileged didn't sweat.

Davies removed his hat revealing a bruised face and eye swollen shut to the stranger.

"And *who* are you?"

"This is … good God, Davies, you look terrible," a surprised McCloud said, then fumbled to move the introductions along and get to the meat of the moment.

"This is the Right Honorable Franklin Ashfield."

"Politician, huh?"

"Correct."

Davies was focused on McCloud, readying himself for the onslaught he knew to be coming.

"A pleasure to meet you as well, inspector," said Ashfield, grinning slightly at Davies's lack of manners and feeling a little of his God-given superiority. He also gave McCloud a look that said, "I now understand what you have to put up with, old boy."

"Oh, right. And you too," said Davies, absently offering a handshake, while making a few more mental notes on the man. Thin blond hair perfectly coiffed, well-manicured, slightly effeminate features. But offset by a body rather thick and barrel-chested -- an odd juxtaposition that would stick with Ifan.

But, finally, the meet.

"Do you want to tell me what the hell this is," snapped McCloud, brandishing the morning paper. The broad letters of the headline proclaiming:

ALLEY GRAFFITI EERLY IDENTICAL TO "RIPPER" MURDERS, IS JACK NOW IN TORONTO? And just below, in slightly smaller type, was the head or the story of Alexander Miller's suicide. Both stories now eclipsed the latest heat-wave death toll, up to 23. The elderly, as usual, but now, the first two children.

"A newspaper? Would you like me to read it to you?" Davies replied with a wry smile.

"Don't be smart with me. I want to know why you let this leak to the press. And don't bother to deny it. I've already spoken to constable Donahue; he told me of the little prank you pulled."

"Well, if you know all this already… I'm sorry, but should he be listening to this?"

Davies had interrupted himself to gesture towards Ashfield, who'd been silently enjoying the obvious dislike the other two had for one another.

"The government," Ashfield gracefully interjected, "has a vested interest if it turns out to be true."

"Well then, at this moment, there is no reason to believe it or not to believe it," Davies offered with a blank expression, looking from one man to the other.

"Then why the hell did you let the press have it? The whole damn city is on edge," yelled McCloud. "The mayor and the chief want your head and are none too happy with me either. Don't think I'm going let you pull me down with you."

"Don't *you* think it's better the people know what's going on?"

"No, no I don't. And neither does the mayor!"

Realizing his temper wasn't going to get him any-where, McCloud sat himself down, let out a sigh and, with an air of forced civility, extended his arms outward, palms open to the sky.

"Tell me then, please, if you have anything to go on at all."

"Possibly," said Davies.

"Possibly? Would you care to let me know so I have something to tell the mayor before he fires me and hangs you!"

"That's a bit dramatic." Davies mumble to himself. Then taking out his notebook, he looked to McCloud as if to, once again, check that Ashfield should be party to this. McCloud just waved him on with a shrug.

"In canvassing the area, I was able to find out that probably three men were heard in the alleyway in the early morning hours when the body of the young woman was dumped there."

"So, she wasn't murdered there?" Ashfield inter-rupted.

Ifan paused, took another looked to McCloud over his notebook, then continued:

"No…. The witness could only hear the men, did not recognize them as local but that one sounded maybe British - or "fancy," as the witness put it. A second witness, at around the same time, saw Little Sean of the onetime Walton Street gang leaving the alleyway followed by two others, but they were obscured from sight. The two accounts and the timing definitely make Little Sean a person we should be interested in."

Ifan pocketed his notebook, crossed his hands in front of him and said no more – except in the look he gave McCloud that asked: Satisfied now?

Ashfield moved to retrieve his hat from the coat rack.

"As fascinating as this is, gentlemen, I must beg your leave so as to express my condolences to Mr. Miller. I'm sure you understand, inspector."

Davies was struck by this sudden shift in Ashfield's demeanor. Once attentive, curious, and even pleasant, he was now rushed and abrupt.

"Oh, and what has happened to Mr. Miller?" Davies asked. "What Mr. Miller?"

McCloud, wishing to ease the way for his visitor, jumped in, only to make the situation more awkward and cumbersome.

"The banker and now MP, John Miller. His son committed suicide yesterday morning, thus the reason I sent for you to deal with the murder."

"His son's name was Alexander, wasn't it?" Davies asked, continuing to observe Ashfield closely.

"Yes, it was." Ashfield replied, looking hung up at the doorway, unsure of how to stay or go, while Davies wanted to hang him up a little longer.

"Sorry to keep you, sir, but aren't you and Mr. Miller on opposite sides of the house?"

"That's one way of putting it."

"I seem to recall there is no love-loss between the two of you and can even recall reading about some quite heated exchanges."

"Indeed. And McCloud, I leave it to you to clarify. Must be on my way. Good day to you, gentlemen. Oh… and Mr. Davies, you should be taking care of that face of yours."

Davies looked on as Ashfield finally made his escape, pausing at the doorway to the street to wipe away a few beads of sweat.

"There is something here you're not telling me," said Davies, turning back to McCloud, now sitting at his desk, and sucking at his teeth, a thing that genuinely bothered Ifan. "And what did he mean you should clarify?"

Shaking his head slightly, McCloud was deliberating how much to confide in Davies or more likely, whether to confide in him at all.

"Ashfield's sister Katherine was secretly engaged to Alexander Miller," he finally relented, shifting papers aimlessly. "Ashfield found out a while ago and had her break it off. There was a row and Alexander was barred from seeing her. That's what Mr. Ashfield came to tell me."

That would be sufficient motive for suicide, I guess," said Davies, turning to look once more at where Ashfield had stopped to wipe his brow.

"I suggest you get on with questioning this Little Sean and finding out what he knows."

"Absolutely, inspector but," said Davies, looking at the newspaper on McCloud's desk, "Alexander Miller committed suicide yesterday at about the same time, or just before the murder victim was found, yes?"

"What of it?"

"It says here, he was – 'totally erratic,' 'frightening,' with 'crazed and wild eyes' - not far from the scene of the murder."

"Sounds like a coincidence to me," said McCloud, rubbing his forehead, wishing to rid himself of Davies.

"I don't believe in coincidences. Can't rule out a murder/suicide. Miller was distraught, rejected, and the engagement broke up. So, he's looking for comfort, and picks up a prostitute. In the course of the evening something goes wrong. He's in a rage and ends up killing her."

"As of right now, we don't have anything connecting these two events. You let me deal with Miller and you concentrate on finding Little Sean."

Ifan had started to move but, glancing over at McCloud's desk was distracted for a moment, then asked, "would you mind if I had Donahue assigned to me? I could use an extra pair of hands."

Something had caught Davies' eye, tucked just under the newspaper was an open file, at the top, the name Alexander Miller. Scanning quickly down the page, he read, *the victim made the sign of a triangle above…*but the rest of the page was obscured.

"Take him." McCloud said. Seeing Davies was snooping his desk, stepped Infront to block him, adding, "oh, get out."

McCloud smiled as he watched Davies leave, he was just handed the opportunity he'd been waiting for.

Davies strode out of McCloud's office with a re-vitalized sense of enthusiasm, a feeling he had almost forgotten. It had always let him know when he was on to something.

"Donahue you're with me," he motioned with a wave and was half-way down the street when the constable, who had to scramble for his notebook and helmet, caught up with him, the day already steamy and the cicadas singing.

"I need you to get me a list of missing persons -- young women, well- to-do young women -- within the last few days."

"Yes, sir. And where will you be?"

"I'm off to the morgue, then to visit Katherine Ashfield."

Donahue stopped in his tracks. He was confused again. Realizing the inspector hadn't stopped, he needed another quick sprint.

"Katherine Ashfield, sir?"

"I also need you to get the word out that I'm looking for Little Sean. He'll be laying low, so shake some trees."

Ifan pulled his watch from his pocket, did some mental arithmetic, then gave Donahue instructions to meet outside of Mickey Doolan's in three hours. Then they split, Donahue off at a trot to where he'd just come from; Ifan heading with sad purpose towards the morgue.

*

Back at division, Donahue was busy pulling records from recent missing persons. *Why Katherine Ashfield? How is questioning her going to help us find a murderer, possibly Jack the Ripper? Has the Inspector gone completely mad? No, of course, he's got a plan, knows something we don't, right?*

McCloud walked up from behind him.

"What are you still doing here? Aren't you supposed to be off with your boyfriend?"

"Excuse me, sir?" Donahue said, looking around to see that he was alone in the room with the inspector.

"Davies. Aren't you supposed to be with him?"

McCloud had moved practically nose to nose.

"I am, sir."

"Doesn't look like it to me."

"It's just… I was asked to…I'm checking missing persons for…"

"I don't give a rat's…," said McCloud, placing his large and heavy hands-on Donahue's shoulders giving the outward appearance of camaraderie but, with enough pressure to indicate: Don't be mistaken. Yes, this is a threat.

"Listen to me. I may have said you're with Davies, but this is the reality. You let me know his every move. I want to know where he goes, who it is he sees and what information he gathers. Got it? You report only to me."

McCloud smiled into Donahue's face, lifting a hand for a light paternal tap to his cheek, then walked off leaving the young officer in a state of outright bewilderment.

He couldn't quite grasp the meaning of what had just transpired, the apparent animosity behind it. Taking another quick look around to make sure nobody had seen the interaction, Donahue breathed out slowly. He was confused as to his loyalty and how he now felt compromised in some way. And in this uncertain and corrupt state of mind, he returned to compiling his list of who'd gone missing.

CHAPTER 11.

Stepping through the basement doors of the hospital morgue, Davies was immediately struck by the powerful smells, like those of formaldehyde. His eyes welled up, but only partly from the chemical onslaught. The smell was always linked to bad memories.

He made his way down a long, drab, damp hallway, stopping in front of a large whitewashed, wooden door with a small square window. He needed it for support when his withdrawal hit him out of nowhere.

"Ffyc!" (fuck!), he whispered.

A light sweat broke on his forehead, everything clenched up at once -- his jaw, his fists, his bowels -- and he started breathing deeply until the moment passed.

When he heard someone coming to the door, he straightened himself up, much like a drunkard does when trying to get one last drink from a bartender who would no longer serve him. The door swung back, and a young orderly looked up from his clipboard to see the strange, sweaty sight of Inspector Ifan Davies quickly standing to attention.

"Oh, it's you, Inspector. Geez you look…um. Well, I haven't seen you here in a long time. This the one you're looking for?"

The orderly pointed with his clipboard towards an enameled table, where a form lay covered with a white sheet.

"A young woman?"

"That's the one. I'm just filing the results. Be sure to check them with Dr. Pennington. The other's down the hall."

"The other?"

"The young man, Miller."

"Right, of course, thank you."

Ifan made it look like he was in a rush and the orderly walked off. The long coats they wore here always reminded him of butchers. All they needed was an apron. They already had the meat.

Ifan pulled back the sheet revealing the young woman's face. Maybe he'd missed something. If not, it would amount to one final look at another senseless act. He removed his hat, ran his fingers through his thinning hair, sighed a deep breath and stood a quiet moment. The sight of death and, in particular, young death always weighed on him, a burning weight that filled his heart, the space between his heart and his stomach and a small spot just below his Adam's apple.

He turned and looked towards the only window in the room, set just below the ceiling but at street level. Busy legs and feet were carrying people about their day, unaware of the sad, lifeless moment he was witnessing.

Improbably, whether by reflection, refraction, or otherworldliness, the diffusing light from the window somehow found the woman's face. Davies thought it beautiful but also that, still, it didn't move. Nothing. Dead is dead.

He placed the sheet back in its place and turned to leave when something stopped him. He stood, absorbed in thought, then returned to uncover her again.

He was still puzzling at something. What had his mind's eye seen? Wasn't sure. He closed his eyes and lightly massaged his forehead. On opening his eyes, from between his fingers, he saw her afresh, and brought his face within inches of hers.

There, at the corners of her mouth, were two small, almost imperceptible, purple-red, crescent-shaped marks curling upward. Ifan pulled back the bottom lip to examine the gum line. Nothing.

*Why did I miss this in the alley? Was I too absorbed by the wounds to the abdomen or was the heat getting to me and my hangover?*

Nodding to himself, Davies covered the body a final time and stepped back to leave a second time, when he heard some singing, or chanting, coming from down the hall, from the cadaver room where bodies were placed after examination.

Ifan went to take a look, pushed open the door and saw two men standing over a body. One he recognized to be John Miller, the MP; the other, obviously a rabbi, who was doing the chanting. The body he knew to be the son Alexander.

"Baruch atah Adonai eloheinu…."

The words were familiar to Davies. King Sol had taught him. They had something to do with…

As the door closed behind Davies, the two men turned, looking both surprised and irritated.

"Can I help you?" said the rabbi, prayer book in hand. "We are in mourning here, preparing the body…"

"Forgive me. I'm inspector Ifan Davies. I was just down the hall. I'm working on another case. I heard the…well, prayer. I'm sorry, very sorry."

"Quite alright," said Miller, extending a hand but clearly wishing to be rid of the intruder. "I'm John Miller. This is my brother Joseph, rabbi. And this…"

"I know, sir. I'm so terribly sorry. I also know this is really not the time and I'll leave you now but, mister Miller, would it be possible to drop by for a short interview? At your earliest convenience, of course."

"For what purpose, Inspector?"

"Trying to help tie up some loose ends."

"Loose ends?"

"Yes, sir."

Miller was irritated but resigned. "Contact my secretary. I'm sure we can arrange something."

Outside, Ifan hurried around the corner and turned up the alley alongside the morgue. Dr. Pennington, the coroner, would have to wait for another visit. He was in a bad sweat and could feel the thickness of his pulse through the collar of his shirt. He leaned back against a wall, breathing violently, eyes clenched tight, willing himself into another fight with withdrawal. *Why the hell did I think I was over this!*

As the pains slowly subsided, he made his way farther up the alley, farther from the busy street. He was looking for any kind of recess or doorway, some cover, to roll himself another "medicinal" cigarette.

He settled on wedging himself into a small gap, barely two feet, between buildings that backed onto the alley, squatted, and pulled out his tin.

He drew the smoke, closed his eyes, and waited for his prescription to take effect, to be calm again.

CHAPTER 12.


"Deliveries are around back."

The ancient and stoic butler would barely look at Davies through the crack in the door he refused to open any wider.

"I'm not here on delivery. Inspector Ifan Davies of the Metropolitan Police."

The grand house and its lush lawns and landscaping had been attractively set up by the Ashfield Family in the city's new and rapidly growing area of Rosedale, an opulent expanse of large stone houses, wide streets, and sidewalks. Very exclusive and very rich.

As he tried to wedge his identification card into the doorway, Davies could hear the butler's exasperated sigh at having to deal with such trivial, unimportant matters along with an equally unimportant and uninteresting person.

"And your business here exactly, sir?"

"I'm wondering - and its inspector - if Miss Ashfield is available to speak with me?

"Sorry, inspector. Miss Katherine isn't receiving visitors today."

But a moment later, from just behind the unblinking servant, a woman's voice…

"It's alright, James. I'll see the inspector."

"But Miss Katherine, your brother gave strict instructions to…"

"I know, I know, but he's not here. Please show the inspector in."

"As you say, miss."

Davies stepped into the vast and lavish entry hall, where, directly in front of him, stepping off a grand and winding staircase came the proud countenance of Katherine Ashfield. He had never seen a room like this, never imagined one like it, either. Massive paintings, very probably originals, filled the clean white walls and, everywhere, fresh-cut flowers billowing out of large vases, some atop black lacquered Chinese cabinets, filled the air with their florid smell.

He quickly stepped towards her, removing his hat, extending his hand. "Forgive the intrusion, miss. I'm Inspector Davies from the Metropol…"

"Yes, so I've heard," she replied, studying Davies' bruised face briefly, saying nothing, then offering her hand in turn. A simple ceremony she understood to be for his sake.

Her features were fine, like her brother's, her blonde hair perfectly done as if she was expecting company at any moment. But her pale blue eyes, puffy and rimmed with redness, betrayed the sadness of loss.

As if she was in a dream - not so much walking as practically floating - Ashfield led him to a small living room off the main hallway followed by the butler's disapproving gaze.

She took a spot on a sofa and motioned him to the chair opposite. This room was far less grand, one would even say homey, with comfortable and well-worn seating, a Persian carpet and walls sparsely decorated with cabinets holding leather-bound books. At one end was a small fireplace that obviously hadn't been lit in months but made Davies uncomfortably hot just looking at it. A few beads of sweat started to form on his forehead, and he started to worry about the effects of the hashish wearing off.

"Another scorcher," offered Davies, a sad unimaginative conversation starter.

"Is it? I hadn't noticed," she replied, casting a languid glance to the window.

"I suppose you're wondering why I'm here."

"No. I'm supposing it has to do with Alexand…"

Her eyes began to well and she dabbed them with a handkerchief. Ifan gave her time to gather herself.

"I'm sorry, every time I even think…"

"Not at all. I'm very sorry, miss…"

With a wave, almost listless, she motioned him to continue.

"It's my understanding you and Mr. Miller were planning to marry?"

"We were, it's true."

"And your brother was against this?"

"Again correct, inspector."

"And why was that?"

"Well, in Franklin's words, 'no stinking kike is going to marry an Ashfield.'" Davies was slightly taken aback. He had heard that word many, many times. It was part of the Ward's lexicon. Even used it himself. But he'd never heard it from a young woman like this, in a place like this.

"So, your brother was aware of your plans to marry?"

"Yes, but we were going to elope. We knew my brother, now the titular head of the family, would never allow it because of Alex being Jewish. Also, my father had stipulated in his will that I reach twenty-one before I marry, to receive my inheritance."

"Miss Ashfield - and, again, apologies - but do you mind me asking your age at the moment?"

"I'll turn twenty next month."

"Well, surely, miss, you realize that, as far as receiving an inheritance, to elope would mean…"

"Yes, I know. I could have fought that in a court of law but, as a woman…well, I'm sure you're aware of my chances there. My brother's also quite petty and vengeful, any blemish on the family name and he can be, let's say… unforgiving."

"I feel I may be missing something here, miss, but, to me, Mr. Miller's, Alex's…um…action… Well, it seems a bit extreme. Why not wait a year, thirteen months, marry as you wished?"

"As I said inspector, my brother can be unforgiving. Sorry, but I'd rather not talk about it anymore. Besides, it's not going to happen, is it? Alexander…. poor Alexander. He wasn't like these other men of high finance. He had the heart of a poet."

"Not like them, how so?"

"He didn't just have the heart of a poet he was a poet. He hated banking. He wished to get away from it, away from his father, as much as I wished to get away from my brother. He wrote every spare moment he had. He was hoping to publish it soon, but his father wouldn't have it. They'd have terrible arguments. He'd threatened to disinherit him."

"Did his father know of the engagement?"

"I'm sure he does now."

"Why would that be?"

"My brother would never allow an opportunity like this to slip past…the chance to wound a rival."

"Wound?"

"Oh yes. My brother and John Miller have hated one another for years. If Franklin had information about Alexander and his plans, especially, if it was he who discovered them and broke them up -- as he did -- he wouldn't hesitate to inflict whatever damage he could on Mr. Miller."

"And why is there this ill-will between your brother and Mr. Miller?"

Ashfield let out a slight laugh, then began to twist her handkerchief tightly in her hands. For a moment, she wouldn't look directly at Davies but slightly off towards the window. Then she said…

"Race. Franklin is a great believer in the new Eugenics movement. The idea that a Jew could sit in Parliament disgusts him. The fact that Mr. Miller has been more than a worthy adversary, infuriates him."

This last outburst seemed to weary the young woman and Davies gently pressed one more question.

"I see. And how was it, miss, that your brother found out about the planned elopement?"

"I don't know."

"One last question," the thought oddly popped into Davies' head. "Did Alexander have an accent?"

"Why do you ask that?"

"Curious."

"Well, he did, sort of. He grew up in England for a short while and had always maintained a slight British accent. I used to tease him about it."

Ashfield was becoming agitated, suddenly distracted as if someone might enter. Davies had been noting her behavior throughout. She spoke succinctly enough, sometimes with a hint of defiance and anger just below the surface. But her mannerisms seemed to drift from lethargy to wispiness to outright fatigue.

She was trying to steady her breath, bowed her head slightly then asked if Davies would mind getting her a glass of water from a decanter on a side table. When he did, she searched her dress pocket for a small vile, shook a few drops into the glass, drained it, tilted her head back and closed her eyes.

"Laudanum?" asked Davies.

"How perceptive, inspector," she said, opening her eyes to focus on him with what he believed to be contempt. He took that as his cue to go, assured her he could find his own way. Just as he was about to leave the room, he turned as if to say something, but Ashfield was in mid-sob, staring blankly out the window.

*

The butler already had the door wide open for him, but Davies had a question when he got there.

"Sir?" the butler anticipated.

"You wouldn't happen to know if your boss has lost a button?"

"A button, sir?"

"Yes, off a coat. Brass."

"Not to my knowledge, sir."

"Well, fine. Nice to meet you, James."

The butler visibly winced as Ifan returned to the heat of the day.

CHAPTER 13.

The sweet and rarefied air of Rosedale was now a good mile distant as Davies crossed into St. John's Ward with just enough time to meet Donahue in front of Doolan's.

The air here was not so sweet, as another day of mind-numbing heat was punishing his delicate state, turning the crowded streets into a sweltering toilet of humanity.

Making his way west along Agnes towards Elizabeth, he spotted a familiar figure darting from stoop to alleyway, in and out of the crowd. In this attempt to conceal himself, Little Sean's staccato-like behavior only made him all the more conspicuous.

*He's on the move*, he thought. Donahue must have gotten the word out.

Sean's probably trying to make his way to Doolan. Davies picked up his pace, hoping to cut him off but, by Elizabeth, the daily bustle of the Ward was in full swing. Progress became slow and difficult, and he lost sight of Sean once, twice then, finally, a third time. He'd meet up with him soon enough.

Fueled by the adrenalin of the chase, Davies continued to feel that sense of purpose he'd thought was long gone.

"GET OUT OF MY WAY!"

The sudden yell from behind snapped Davies out of his reverie and he turned to see Sean running down the middle of Elizabeth, dodging and desperate. He was being chased by a man whose face was obscured with a bandana, only his eyes visible.

Without thinking, he jumped into the street.

"Sean! Stop!"

Sean came to a halt less than ten feet from him, scanned left and right for his best escape, then took a look behind him. Right on him, was the assailant who, without breaking stride, lifted a pistol from his side and dropped Sean with a single shot between the eyes.

As Sean crumbled to the ground, the shooter passed within inches of a dumb-struck Davies who stood transfixed for a moment, he'd never see eyes like those of the killer's, one brown and one blue.

Snapping out of it, Davies turned to see the as-sassin disappear into a shocked and screaming crowd. He had the distinct feeling he was yelling but, with the ringing in his ears, couldn't be sure. People seemed to be moving in slow motion and, while they scattered at first, some were now inching their way back to stare at a lifeless man.

In the distance, the sound of police whistles and, moments later, uniforms breaking through the crowd. The first two of these, noting a dazed inspector wiping at blood splatters on his clothes, checked if he'd been hurt. He waved them off, pointing them in the direction the murderer had fled, while giving them the scant description - a white guy, ratty dark jacket, over a dark blue shirt - he could muster.

He stumbled towards an alley off Elizabeth to collect himself, leaned back against a wall and raised his face to the sky, a strip of brilliant blue between the buildings.

"Jesus Christ! Little Sean," he muttered, shaking his head.

Sean Hackett had been with Mickey and him since the beginning, since the early days of the Walton Street Gang, some thirty years or more back. He and Mickey had been fourteen, already in the "employ" of Mama, when they'd first run into the short, scrawny kid, only twelve. They took him under their wing. He'd shot up over the next couple of years, but the nickname had stuck. They'd become Mama's eyes and ears and, if needed her mules and muscles.  Boy, they were a fearsome sight.

Mama knew the value of these little urchins she fed and sheltered. Mostly, they were the boys and girls of the Ward; others were runaways. All of them were groomed for their particular talents--the boys as fighters, cruel and brutal but most of all, loyal. The girls? To be pretty, to please, to satisfy.

The sound of an ambulance arriving, along with the shouts from constables trying to clear a path, brought him back to the present. Stepping out of the alley, he headed for Doolan's, now the bearer of sad news…

CHAPTER 14.

Working through the missing persons' reports, Donahue had been frustrated to find that most were incomplete or had never been followed up on. Nothing that recent, except for a couple of the usual runaways, and certainly nothing on young women connected to well-off families.

Still, he'd come up with a few names he could track down that might be of some interest to the inspector, whom he now had just enough time to meet.

As Donahue made his exit, he could feel McCloud's eyes on his back and his guts churn slightly. What was he supposed to do? Davies was now his partner, and you don't spy on your partner. *Yes, he was also a bit of an asshole. Had already got me in trouble.*

Donahue was still working on how he was going to handle this when he came up on Davies pacing in front of Doolan's, finishing a cigarette. Even from a distance, he could tell Davies was agitated and, as he drew closer, blood-spattered as well.

"Sir! Are you alright?"

Davies looked up from his thoughts, then quickly tossed his butt.

"I'm fine. Let's get to this."

There was little light coming from the bar below and, from the sound of it, about the same amount of activity. The end of work-day crush was still hours away and three of Doolan's men lounging about a rear table couldn't help but notice a uniform was one of the two newcomers. Mickey stepped out from behind the bar, a baleful grin on his face.

"It's like you never learn, Ifan."

"Always been my problem."

"I see you've brought reinforcements."

"The lad's fierce. I wouldn't test him if I were you."

Davies wasn't giving any ground, which prompted a nervous glance from Donahue. Mickey had noticed.

"Relax, son. I'm not stupid enough to make trouble with the local constabulary. But you, Ifan, now that's another matter, a personal matter."

"You should have told me where Sean was."

"Like I told you…"

Davies locked eyes with Doolan.

"It might've saved his life."

Doolan's sardonic composure disappeared and was replaced by a deadly seriousness that chilled the room.

"What the fook are you sayin'?"

"Sean was just gunned down in the middle of Elizabeth, less than half hour ago. He's dead."

"Bullshit!"

"Happened right in front of me."

"You're lyin'"

"Mickey, look! I'm wearing his blood"

The sheer earnestness on Davies' face, the pleading in his voice, finally sold Doolan on the horrible truth. He clenched his fists and started sliding towards rage.

"Who?"

"His face was covered, and he was moving too fast for me."

Doolan had run around the corner of the bar, reached under, and pulled out his hand-carved shillelagh, a menacing cudgel made of solid oak. His men snapped out of their chairs.

"The kikes! Huh? The coloureds?

"No."

"Come on, lads, arm yourselves!"

"Mickey!" Ifan yelled in a voice that was as urgent as it was sharp, stepping up to go chest-to-chest with

Doolan. Sensing imminent danger, Donahue started eyeing one gang member to the next.

"You gettin' in my way copper?"

"Ya, I'm gettin' in your way."

The two faced one another in silence for several moments before Ifan slowly lifted both hands to Mickey's shoulders, resting them with a gentle firmness, a quiet honest gesture meant to convey his understanding. Dropping his chin to his chest, Doolan stood silent a few moments more, took a step back, gave Davies two pats on the heart, then turned to the bar where he slammed down his weapon.

Then, with a sudden wail of anger and hurt, he tried yanking the massive countertop off its anchors and, failing that, dropped his head to the bar with a faint sob.

"Mickey, tell me what you know. What was Sean up to?"

"Nothin'."

"He's gone, Mickey. Who or what are you protecting?"

"He didn't tell me nothin.' Just that he made a few easy bucks movin' something for some rich gent."

"He say who this might have been?"

"Nah."

This was an odd and uncomfortable scene for Donahue, befuddled by the apparent tenderness between these two since, only the previous night, Doolan had been pissing on the inspector's head.

"Mickey, come on," Davies continued pressing, hoping to jog Doolan's memory. "Anything. Anything Sean might've said about this guy. Anything at all."

"I don't know, but I think Sean said the gent spoke with an accent."

"Are you meaning British, maybe upper-class?"

"Yeah, fancy-like. I think that's what he said. The gent was waving a good chunk of change under Sean's nose."

Micky paused for a moment, biting his lower lip, weighing a thought. Tell Davies or not to tell the Davies seemed to be playing out in the man. Ifan recognizing Doolan's struggle and offered one final nudge:

"Please, Mickey."

"Look, Sean was on hard times. I couldn't carry him no more. Plus, his health and age, I just couldn't."

"So, he wouldn't have been averse to some shady dealings."

"Those in want never are."

Ifan nodded, scribbled down a few notes, then looked to Donahue who'd been watching the exchange closely.

"Mickey, cheers," he said, waving his notebook as he headed for the steps.

"Ifan! Keep your wits about ya, mate. You know the gentry. They'll fook ya."

As the two nodded to one another, it was as if a lifetime had just passed between them, the ghosts of which neither wished to dredge up. At least, not without a bottle of whisky between them.

CHAPTER 15.

Walking back into division, Davies told Donahue to make himself scarce until he was ready to get out of there. He knew there'd be words with McCloud and didn't want the constable getting caught in the cross-fire. Donahue objected, saying he could manage the inspector and that, besides, they were partners now.

Davies had to smile, gave Donahue a sideways glance and a pat on the shoulder and assured: "No, you go. But thanks for the back-up."

Davies then wheeled open the door to McCloud's office and strode in, startling the inspector who'd been hunched over a file on his desk.

"Jesus Christ, haven't you ever heard of knock-ing!"

"I thought it best I just come right in and give you shitty news before you start hollering for my head." Davies answered back. "And, before you start, I had nothing to do with it."

Davies, who'd expected McCloud to start yelling at the get-go, had decided he'd be the one to set things in motion and was a little taken aback when McCloud leaned back in his chair with a slight grin on his face.

"Had nothing to do with it, huh?"

"No, sir."

"So, it wasn't you who decided to visit Franklin Ashfield's sister? The MP must have got the name wrong."

"Oh, that. Yes, I visited her. I thought you'd be wanting to talk about the daylight murder of Sean Hackett in the middle of Elizabeth Street." Davies had been thinking quickly there, figuring a good offence would be a good defense -- or, at least, catch McCloud off guard, which he could see he had. For one thing, he'd obviously yet to file his report on that.

"What the hell are you talking about?" McCloud growled, forgetting all about the Ashfields and rising to Davies' bait. "Are you talking about that two-bit hoodlum, the Wee Sean."

"I'll file the report later. Right now, I need an autopsy on Hackett to determine what caliber weapon was used."

"And what does this have to do with the murder of a prostitute?"

"She wasn't a prostitute, that's for certain. She was murdered, but not where she lay. And Hackett was mixed up in it somehow and now he's dead."

Davies had spit that out rapid-fire and, with the intention of giving McCloud no time to think or respond, turned to leave.

"Not so fast!" snapped McCloud, rising to lean hard with his fists into the top of the desk. "I look forward to your report. I'm sure it will be most edifying. But if you ever decide to visit an MP or any of their family members again, even on police business, without permission, you'll be tossed out of the force and, believe me, you'll never have a moment's peace. DO YOU HEAR ME?"

While McCloud's face was turning various shades of red, Davies was backing out the door, waving his so long and smiling sarcastically when he almost bumped into Donahue.

"Everything alright, sir?"

"Boy was he ever angry at you. Not to worry, though, I fixed it for you."

Donahue took a quick glance through the glass partition to see McCloud launching into another of his rants, then ran after Davies, sputtering for some assurance the inspector had been only joking.

Just before the exit, Davies decided he needed the toilet and told Donahue to wait outside. Inside the washroom, Davies took a stall, sat down hard, and wiped his forehead into his sleeve. It had been a few hours since he had had a puff of medicine, the last being just before entering Doolan's. He reached for his tin -- time to keep the shakes at bay.

Donahue was pacing the sidewalk outside Division, watching people stroll by. *They don't know or, they don't care a young woman was murdered.*

Sticking his hands in his pockets and staring down at his shoes he shook his head at his own thoughts when Davies came bounding down the steps. A cooler evening was settling in, bringing some long-awaited relief for the city.

"Ready to go, son?"

"To go where?"

"Let's get some Chop Suey, huh?"

*

At a small table in one of the new Chinese restaurants that had been popping up in the Ward, Donahue looked around with the uneasy realization that they were the only white folks in the place.

"Relax, son, nobody's gonna bite you."

"I've just never been in… I've never eaten this kind of… food."

A waiter briskly brought over a pot of tea with two small ceramic cups. Davies nodded thanks, took to handling the pouring and ordered two plates of chop suey.

And, in answer to Donahue's quizzical look, added: "It's a fried dish with meat, egg and vegetables. It's terrific -- and cheap."

After a careful taste of tea, Donahue decided he'd take the moment to tiptoe into a question that had been gnawing at him since they were in Doolan's.

"So, you Doolan and this Sean were all friends?"

"Kind of, ya."

"Well, I knew you had grown up rough and had some run-ins with the law but..."

Ifan, looking over his cup, was staring directly into the officer's eyes. Donahue was staring right back, feeling the burden of years reflected back. He knew that the answer -- if there was going to be one -- could be long and complicated. Ifan took another sip, placed his cup on the table and sat back in his chair. He was touched by the earnestness.

"We were all orphans. Well, Sean and me. Mickey just left when his father beat him for the last time. Sean -- and we called him Little Sean -- never knew his folks. My father, too, was violent and a drunk. My earliest, my only memories of him are of him beating my mum after coming home drunk. My mum died when I was about five and then I got passed from family member to family member, but none could afford to keep me and, I ended up in St. John's orphanage where I met Sean. At thirteen, we ran away out of that hell-hole."

"And how'd you meet Doolan?"

"Hunger."

"I don't understand."

"Well, Sean and me, we didn't do so well out there. We did a bit of thieving but, mostly, our bellies were empty, sleeping anywhere we could, a bit of shelter out of the elements. It was always dangerous.

"One day, we're both pretty hungry and trying to figure a way of gettin' some food. We'd staked out a grocery on Elizabeth and were waiting 'til the owner got distracted to make our move when we notice this rough looking kid, about our age, scoping us.

"It was pissing me off. I thought he was moving in on our action, so I went up to him to tell him to buzz off. He just grinned at me and said, 'Come on, you guys wanna to meet someone.' That's how we met Mama, how the Walton Street Gang was born."

As his story trailed off, so had Ifan. He was looking past Donahue, focused on a Chinese lantern hanging in a lonely little window that opened on the alley. He closed his eyes, took a deep breath. On his return, he shook his head and pulled out his notebook, looking like a new man. Donahue took the cue and got his notebook out as well.

Davies wanted to know what Donahue had come up with from missing persons, to which he replied, 'very little,' then turned over what he had gathered.

"I want you to follow up on those names first thing tomorrow, so we can rule them out for sure. I'll be paying the Right Honorable John Miller a visit."

"Sir? What does Mr. Miller have to do with this case?"

"Possibly nothing."

"Possibly?"

Davies was giving nothing more away. Besides, the food had arrived, and Ifan had to have a slight laugh at Donahue's obvious puzzlement over chopsticks. He offered to show him how it was done, avoiding any further questions.

"My gosh this is good," enthused Donahue, realizing he hadn't eaten all day and now attacking his food.

"See, nothing to be afraid of," smiled Davies, realizing that other than that one candy he'd got from the King, this would be the first thing he'd eaten in three days. As they ate, the two men fell into silence.

CHAPTER 16.

Ifan was trying to fall asleep, but his mind persisted in racing through the events of the past two days. There'd been a lot of them.

*I'm working the case. McCloud's a dick. Things are going well. That Donahue kids alright. I got to eat more regularly. Damn it, Sean! I wish I wasn't so hungover at that young woman's murder scene. No, we're making progress.*

The effects of his physical withdrawal were amplifying all of his insecurities. He was restless, his muscles twitched, his body was bathed in sweat. He'd feel like he was suffocating and kick off his sheets, only to pull them right back when the sting of the air brought on shivers. This wrestling between mind and body, sheets, and air lasted hours.

Nights were always long when coming off the booze. There was simply nothing there to distract him from obsessing over just how horrible he felt. And this night was particularly difficult since, every time he closed his eyes, he'd see Sean's head explode and would jerk upright.

He tried smoking just enough hash to fall asleep, get through the rest of the night, but the drug would fizzle away in his restlessness.

If the nights were hard coming off the booze, the mornings were next to impossible. There would always be a lot of dead-time between his actual waking and moving towards getting something done.

Most days just started out of habit -- a way to get out of his head, away from his thoughts. Most times, one day after the next, he'd wake up feeling more exhausted than the night before, always wondering why the hell he continued to do this to himself. He couldn't even remember his reasons for drinking anymore.

The drink itself had become his tormentor.

Looking into his mirror, he'd become used to feeling the sting of age and regret. All he'd see would be a youth, long past, a future that offered little comfort, and little of a sense of self-worth. Today, though, he was able to question his reflection.

*These last two days? Haven't had a drink. Wanted one several times, just never got there. Today, I'm gonna try to not even think of having one. I'm doing good work. I've got some purpose. I feel something coming.*

What he didn't feel coming as he rolled the day's first cigarette – almost surprising himself with the realization -- was the urge to sprinkle in a little hashish.

Another surprise: His hands weren't shaking.

Despite his mostly sleepless night, he was going to try seeing John Miller. He hadn't made an appointment like he was supposed to but was hoping his timing was right. Besides, it was going be a good day.

He walked out into a bright and, for a change, pleasant morning, the sluggish citizenry slowly coming to life, the normal din of the streets just beginning. He filled his lungs, feeling the great fog starting to lift.

Stepping into the expansive foyer of the building that housed Miller's constituency offices, Davies checked out the directory, then headed for the large marble staircase. It was early enough that few people were about, not even the secretary in Miller's outer office. He strode across the room and knocked.

Hearing a gruff, "Enter!" Davies let himself into a spacious bright room where Miller was hunched over some papers at an immense desk in front of large bay windows that looked out across the lake and the Toronto islands.

"Miss Smith, I'll need you to contact..."

When Davies cleared his throat. Miller was slightly startled. Definitely not his secretary.

"Who the h...Oh, it's you, inspector. Davies, am I right? Did we have an appointment this morning? I don't recall my secretary informing me of..."

"Very sorry, sir. I didn't make an appointment and I don't mean to barge in, but I only have a few questions and thought it best to be a as discreet as possible."

'Discreet' had been a good choice of words, somehow making the interruption ...agreeable. Miller nodded he was willing to oblige.

"Thank you, sir. To start, I understand you lived in England for a time?"

"Yes, in London, but that was years ago."

"Alexander grew up there?"

'No, just a couple of years. I was working for the house of Morgan."

"And when was that?"

"Must be over ten years ago now. Alex was ten or eleven when we left."

Davies leaned forward, doing some mental arithmetic. "So, you would have heard all about the White Chapel murders?"

"Couldn't get away from it. They were all over the papers."

"Probably made quite the impression on a young boy."

"Yes, I'm sure it did."

"Were you aware that your son was engaged to Katherine Ashfield?"

"Well, it wasn't a formal engagement, more of a silly whim. They knew the marriage could never occur."

"And why would that be?"

Davies watched as Miller waved the notion of the engagement away like some pesky fly about his head. His absolute and total dismissal of the conceit left no doubt in Davies' mind that Alexander and Katherine never had a chance.

"So, you knew of this informal, let's say, promise the two had made to one another. Do you mind telling me when it was that you became aware of their plans?"

"Exactly when I couldn't say."

"Approximately."

"Approximately, I would say, a week before Alex…"

Miller's formal MP demeanor crumbled at a memory that was still far too fresh.

"Excuse me, I find it hard to discuss."

"Of course. Just one more question?"

Miller, dabbing the corner of his eye with a forefinger, slowly nodded his consent. "Did you and your son have a disagreement or quarrel about the engagement before the morning he took his life?"

"Fathers and Sons often have disagreements. What of it? What does that have to do with anything?"

"Sir, I'm merely trying to determine your son's state of mind before he acted."

"Are you suggesting that I'm somehow to blame for my son's suicide? Get the hell out of my office or I'll have you removed."

Miller had bolted up from his chair, face reddening and his voice rising to a level that brought his bewildered secretary rushing.

"Are you alright, sir? Oh, I didn't realize you were…Did you have an appointment, sir?"

"The gentleman was just leaving, Miss Smith."

"That I am. Sorry for the intrusion."

And as Davies closed the door behind him, he could hear Miller shout, "McCloud will hear about this!"

CHAPTER 17.

It had been a morning like no other for Donahue and he was exhausted, both physically and emotionally. By twists and turns, it had been occasionally uplifting but also depressing, even heart-wrenching.

He'd cycled through the city, following up on missing persons that he'd determined, despite frustratingly incomplete files.

He had seven on his list, all of them more or less runaways, and his very first call had been encouraging in that the missing girl, herself, answered the door. The family hadn't thought or bothered to notify the police and, while Donahue was annoyed, he decided there was no point in chastisement. What was he going to say: Next time, let us know?

A second young woman had also thought better of her adventure and returned home, while another turned out to be living with an aunt in Montreal.

Another woman unraveled at yet another constable at her door. She screamed at Donahue that they had never found the cause of her daughter's death. She told him to clear off.

When he got back to his bike, he walked it for about fifty feet, resting it up against a tree, then stood a few minutes to simply watch the world go by. He decided people weren't caring enough.

Two hours later, Donahue finally closed his notebook. His very low expectations for any sort of new lead had been met precisely.

Of the final three that could still be regarded as missing, one was now twenty-eight and gone for almost three years. This was a line to scratch out in his notebook; to the others… well, what does anybody think when a constable makes his way up your stoop? A brief flash of almost forgotten hope, followed by a bracing for the worst and the sudden, sickening dread of being asked to come to the morgue.

Back at division, Davies had yet to show so Donahue headed back to missing persons, pulling the files that he, himself, had just now "resolved," and adding some missing information he'd collected to others.

He was about to go back to look up a few files he decided he might've originally dismissed when some commotion started up at the desk up front. He knew Eddie McDermott was at the post, the only constable in division younger, and greener, than he was. Maybe he should lend a hand.

As Donahue made his way from the filing cabinets in the rear, he became aware of some booming, privileged voice pressuring a frustrated young officer. This, he would soon learn, was Donald Sparks, of Sparks financial holdings and savings, one of the largest federal lobbyists in the country. With him was the shrinking presence of his wife, Myrtle, who could only look nervously about in some apology for her husband's manner.

"As I've told you already, I want action. Answers! I pay your salary, son."

Eddie sputtered out, "I realize it may be difficult to…"

"Who is your superior here? It's McCloud isn't it?"

"Yes, sir, but he's…"

"He's what? And don't you say unavailable or I'll…"

Donahue, unintimidated by the bluster, chose that moment to step in.

"Or you'll what, sir? Continue to verbally assail an officer of the law?"

Only slightly taken aback, Sparks responded with, "Apologies. I wouldn't, It's just that…"

"Alright, sir and what is it we can do for you? Inspector McCloud is busy with a murder investigation."

"Ah yes, of course, the whole nasty Ripper business, yes…"

"And how might we help, sir?"

Donahue asked again, slipping his young colleague a sideways glance that said putting on his best service manner like this was something the rich felt most comfortable with.

"Well, my daughter has gone missing."

"Sorry to hear that. I'm sure it will all be fine. So, you're here then to file a missing person's report?"

"No… I mean, well, I guess I am."

Sparks, rarely experiencing such a forthright and unimpressed demeanor in a subordinate, had been further disarmed.

As Donahue started filling in the required form… Eugenia Sparks, just turned twenty-one, light brown hair, a mole on her right cheek, five foot three inches tall…his heart suddenly missed a beat. He began to breathe rapidly, his palms starting to sweat. This was precisely the profile he'd been dealing with all morning. By no means was it a certainty but definitely a very good a match. Stay calm, get hold. Ask something!

"And when did she go missing, sir?"

"Well, that's the thing. We don't really know. Eugenia was supposed to have disembarked in Southampton as of today, sometime early-afternoon, Greenwich time. She was to telegraph us immediately upon arrival but hasn't done so. That was three or four hours ago now! We've tried, both here and Southampton, but no one from the cruise-line has been very helpful. Making…we're both very distraught."

Sparks motioned to his wife, standing by demurely, who nodded in the affirmative that she too was indeed suffering.

"So, when did you last see her?"

"That would be the morning of the 5th, she had an early train to Montreal the day of her evening sailing."

"And she was traveling alone?"

"Yes. I should have insisted she travel with a chaperone but, it's all the fashion now to let young daughters have experiences on their own."

Sparks' voice struck a paternal chord that Donahue hadn't heard in the man, almost making him warm to him.

As the Sparks readied to leave, Donahue offered them further assurances that all would turn out well... that he would personally bring this to McCloud's attention, that he would get back to them very soon.

He was also facing growing doubt that his assurances weren't misplaced, and it was with a mix of dismay and excitement that he now awaited Davies' arrival. He wasn't the only one waiting

"Where the hell is Davies, constable?" McCloud bellowed from about ten feet off, on the prowl and well into his normal agitated state. "Did I order you to keep an eye on him or not, huh?"

"I didn't realize you wanted me to sleep with him," said Donahue, without thinking, his mind in several places at once. "Maybe I should have been waiting outside his door this morning with a cup of coffee."

"Don't get smart with me, Donahue, or you'll be handing out Sunday observance tickets."

"Protestant Sundays, huh! That Lord's Day Act is..."

"Is what son?"

McCloud was leaning into Donahue with all the implied threat he could muster into those three words when Davies suddenly provided a welcomed reprieve.

"I hope you two weren't talking about me behind my back," he announced, looking better and more energetic than both McCloud and Donahue had seen in days -- apart from the bruises Doolan left.

"You two, in my office, NOW!" McCloud snapped, storming off in a manner that, by now, seemed almost comical to both. As Davies moved to follow, Donahue stopped him with a hand to his elbow.

"Inspector, I think I've found something."

"Go on!"

"Could be. A very possible lead, I believe."

"Excellent. Let's get this done first."

Two steps into McCloud's office, Davies came to a sudden stop because of yet another face to face with Franklin Ashfield, perched on the edge of McCloud's desk, arms crossed. Donahue couldn't help but run into

Davies from behind, causing the two to slightly stumble into the room.

"Nice to see you have such a talented set of clowns working on one of the highest profile cases this city has ever seen," Ashfield said, turning to addressing McCloud over his shoulder.

"Sorry sir, my fault," Donahue, jumped in to cover.

"Come in and close the door," said McCloud, eyes rolling to the ceiling.

Ashfield and Davies had already exchanged those nods with that cool cordiality reserved for use between class divides, each retaining his prejudice towards the other.

"Inspector Davies," McCloud resumed, preparing to set out in a formal manner, "I charged you with the investigation of the young prostitute found murdered in the Ward now three days gone, is that correct?"

"Hmmm, not exactly, sir. It was two days ago. And it was only yesterday, right here, that I told you she wasn't a prostitute and that she had been murdered elsewhere and moved there."

'Well, yes. But you did assure me that you were following a line of inquiry that you believed would give us some answers."

"Yes, sir. But that line of inquiry, as you also know, died with Sean Hackett."

McCloud had at least tried to keep matters cordial, upbeat, but obviously needed some ammunition. Donahue had been wondering when the axe might fall.

"Well, I just wanted to let you know that I received a letter today from the killer, mocking our investigation and the whole Metropolitan Police department. He also sent the letter to the newspapers. He's calling himself Jack the Ripper!"

Getting more wound up with every word McCloud needed to take a breath to keep his temper in check. As much as McCloud wanted to see the fall of the *great* Ifan Davies, he was also starting to take a lot of heat from the mayor, who didn't like the attention of the papers. He needed to rein him in.

"Can you give me one good reason to keep you on this case, Davies?"

Davies calmly offered: "It's a blunder."

"A blunder how?"

"Our man's worried we're losing interest, the public's losing interest.  He's running scared."

Ashfield suddenly let out a laugh, turning to McCloud in disbelief. "That's ridiculous! Sorry to interrupt, gentlemen, but how can you even know that?"

"The killer knows that the police don't buy the Ripper business. He -- and I do assume the killer is a he -- is going to great lengths to persuade the general public that he is, in fact, the Ripper."

But the evidence…" McCloud started up, only to be cut off by Davies.

"There is no evidence he's the Ripper. What was left for us was a staged scene and, these letters, a stolen playbook probably copied out of old newspapers. The killer intends to keep the attention of the public diverted and have us chase ghosts. I do apologize but, what pieces of this puzzle I do have, I'm not ready to divulge to a government supervisor putting pressure on us to come up with a fairy-tale to spoon feed the public, and his political masters."

"Now wait a moment, Davies. This is a respected Member of Parliament. You can't just…"

"No, no, it's alright McCloud," Ashfield interjected. "Inspector Davies is correct. It must appear that way with my presence here so often. From now on, I'll conduct my inquiries through the proper channels. We can't have a perception of government interference with our police. Arms' length and all that, you know."

Ashfield collected his hat and walking stick, bid McCloud good day, then nodded to both Davies and Donahue in a deferential way that came across as sarcasm.

Davies stopped him at the door with a final question.

"Before you leave, sir. I was just wondering about your buttons."

"My buttons?"

"Yes, I noticed them last time you were here. They're very distinctive. Do you have them made for you?"

"Actually, they're made for the members of a club."

"A club?"

"More, let's say, a society of gentlemen."

"Was Alexander Miller a part of this *society* club?" Davies pressed, still hanging Ashfield up at the door and clearly getting agitated.

"What are you leading at," chimed in McCloud.

"Miller made the sign of a triangle over his head just before he shot himself, I find that terribly interesting."

"No, he was not a part of our society. That is surprising though. I can say however, that your superior here and the Mayor are also members."

"What about the Chief?" Davies half-heartedly joked.

"No, not him," retorted Ashfield, in what Davies felt to be a clipped, all-too serious tone.

During this exchange, McCloud had got up from behind his desk to better display his jacket for Davies. Yes, same buttons, stamped with that same design of a triangle.

With another nod to everyone, Ashfield finally made his way out, which is when Davies turned an inquisitive look towards McCloud.

"When did you join a society club?"

"I was asked. More importantly, how did you know Miller had made that sign?"

"It was in your report, I saw the file when it was sitting on your desk."

McCloud looked like he was about to explode but seeing Donahue in the room thought better of it.

"We'll continue this later but know this, Alexander Miller was a disturbed and mixed-up young man who didn't know what he was saying or doing."

Davies signaled Donahue, frozen in disbelief at all he had just witnessed, towards the door.

"Are we done here? Are we free to continue our work?"

"You are an insubordinate prick you know, Davies. Yes, we're done, get out. And know this: I will feed you to the sharks if you mess with me."

"Noted."

On the way out, Davies called back over his shoulder. "Oh, you'll be hearing from John Miller about me. Just thought I'd let you know." He'd timed it to the closing of the door.

As they headed down the steps of division, Donahue could barely contain himself.

"So, Jimmy, let's hear what you have."

"Well, my morning was a wash-out but, just after noon, a couple turned up at division to report their daughter missing. Eugenia Sparks. She was supposed to take a train to Montreal on the fifth and to sail to England the same night but hadn't turned up."

"Supposed to take the train?"

"Yes. She was traveling alone, so her parents have no idea if she even left the city."

"And they are?"

"The parents are Donald and, I think, Myrtle Sparks. He's big in banking."

"I'm aware of him."

"She, the daughter Eugenia… her description's a good match with our Jane Doe. Fits in most ways. I'd say fits all we're looking for, best we have so far."

The news excited Davies, too, but that was mostly under wraps. He had definitely admired Donahue's discretion during whatever that was with McCloud and, for that, offered a warm smile and a couple of hefty pats on the shoulder.

"Okay, look, I'm headed over to the morgue to get a detailed report. You go to the steam ship offices, ask for the passenger manifest, and make sure the Sparks girl boarded. If you've got time, see what you can find out at the train station."

Davies pulled out his watch, gave it a tap and a listen.

"After that, Doolan's again. Let's say 3 p.m. I'll go directly inside. I got to talk to Mickey."

"Sir, if I may?"

"Shoot."

"Why aren't we buying the stuff about the Ripper? How can you tell the scene was staged?"

"A little theatre for Ashfield," Davies said, again patting Donahue on the shoulder, then walked off leaving the constable as perplexed as ever.

CHAPTER 18.

Davies needed a quick smoke before heading into the morgue, a moment to roll some thoughts around.

Donahue's discovery about the Sparks girl had been encouraging, the first real break since learning King Sol had seen Sean coming out of the alley, sometime in the early morning of the day before the young woman was discovered.

There was also the button he'd found there the next day. If that was really a clue -- and he had convinced himself it was – it was complicated by learning a whole society of people wore the same distinct button. There was something about it, though; something about Ashfield, too, that he couldn't quite put his finger on. The thought was still gnawing at him as he stepped into the morgue.

The coroner's office was a bleak, messy room with a lonely window covered in dirt and grime that no sunlight ever penetrated. Every counter, desk and chair, even flat surfaces, was piled high with a clutter of files, books, and medical instruments. At a desk at the back, virtually buried alive, Davies could pick out the compact body and bald head of Dr. Jack Pennington.

The little man pushed his round wire spectacles up on his forehead and held a piece of paper as close as he could to his eyes. Finally deciphering something, he licked the tip of his nub of a pencil and jotted a note in a little book.

"I could never understand," Davies announced his presence, "how you ever find anything in this room, let alone figure out cause of death or murder weapons."

The bald head looked up, squinting, smiling.

"I bet I know what you're here for, you no-good saloon hustler."

"Oh, you think, do you, you blind miscreant card cheat?"

"Better that than a no-talent beat cop who couldn't find Jack the Ripper."

"God, not you too!"

"Hah. Good for you! I was worried you'd swallowed that malarky."

"Nah, I just let the press chatter. I also like watching McCloud lose his mind dealing with the Mayor."

"A dangerous game, kid."

"Maybe, old man."

To anyone watching these two together, the great respect and affection they held for one another would be clearly obvious.

Pennington got up from his desk, pulled a file from a pile and headed towards Davies. As always, he was wearing a crisp white lab coat over disheveled clothing, the juxtaposition of which was always comforting to

Ifan. It was as if a bum had walked in off the street, pretending he was a doctor.

Ifan began to flip through the report, while Pennington started up with the commentary.

"As you can see, the girl was murdered somewhere else, a good few-hours, maybe even a day, before she was placed in the alley. There were ligature marks, as well as rope burns on her wrists and her ankles, consistent with being tied up. They're older than her other wounds, so, I can assume she was held captive for some time. Wherever she was held, it was without ventilation or water, again an assumption. She was quite dehydrated. In this heat wave, she couldn't have lasted too long.  Also, whoever removed her organs didn't know what they were doing."

"How so?"

"They hacked away like an amateur butcher. Actually, a butcher would have greater skill. This person left portions of organs behind, ragged edges. It looks like it was a hurried job, an afterthought. The killer is improvising, he didn't use a scalpel, something more like a hunting or carving knife. The poor thing was a mess. Wherever this took place, there's going to be a lot of blood."

"Cause of death?"

"Even though her throat was slit, it wasn't the cause of death. The body was in such bad shape, if I had to give you an answer, I'd say heat and dehydration were the cause.

"But you're not sure."

Pennington had removed his glasses to try and clean the lenses with a corner of his lab coat. He held them up to what little light there was from the window to check his work, found he had only smeared the smudges around and gave up. With a disgruntled huff, he hooked the frames back around his ears and pointed to a place on the page.

Ifan read in silence, taking in the information with a deep breath. Rubbing his forehead, he handed the file back to Pennington, their eyes meeting, a sadness passing between the two.

"She was possibly raped?"

"I can't be sure of that. Her stomach, womb and sexual organs were attacked with such extreme rage. If we are to believe Dr. Freud, more likely, a sign of sexual impotence."

Pennington nodded and headed back to his desk to pull another file off the stack.

"You'll want to see this as well. Little Sean's report. And Ifan, I'm sorry. I know you two went back some. We think, from the size of the wound, it was a Smith and Wesson, type 38, but, without the slug, we can't be sure."

"Pretty common gun," Ifan said quietly, giving the file a cursory glance before handing it back, certain there'd be no surprises coming there.

He thanked his old friend for his work and, after a few half-hearted parting quips, headed back into the streets, where whatever respite there'd been from a cool overnight, was now a distant memory.

CHAPTER 19.

At the steam ship office, Donahue was having a difficult time with a young clerk who was refusing him access to the passenger manifest he'd requested. The thin young man had a pinched face with a sharp nose that he seemed intent on keeping elevated in order to look down past. To Donahue, it looked like a comical impression of someone who had just smelled shit.

"I assure you," Donahue renewed his pursuit, "there's absolutely no question of liability for the company. I only want to clarify that a passenger had actually embarked. I'm presuming you do note if people are on board or not, in case of shipwreck or other unforeseen calamity."

"Constable, again, we are simply not in the habit of giving out the personal information of our guests."

Donahue knew this was not true, that the clerk was only being obstinate to flex some kind of power. So, he opted to appeal to the clerk's sympathy, rather than point out the fact, risking an argument.

"And rightfully so. But this is in aid of a missing person investigation. The family here is absolutely distraught."

The clerk crinkled his nose and, in a motion filled with the drama of exhaustion for Donahue's benefit, well, he was young and good looking, pulled a large ledger from a shelf behind him.

"And the name again?"

"Sparks. Eugenia Sparks."

"Q, R, S… Sparks. Yes, here we are, Eugenia Sparks. Ship sailed out of Montreal on the 5th. And no. She had a ticket but, according to our records, never made it, never boarded."

"You're sure?"

"My dear constable, we are meticulous in our attention to detail. Not only do we have a boarding check, but the room was also entered and checked during boarding, checked again after departure and once more at disembarking, as you can see."

The clerk had turned the ledger around towards Donahue to review. Donahue felt compelled to make a note, but all he could think to write was: "Never on boat!!"

And what he now wanted to know was why the Sparks parents - the father, at least - hadn't seen, hadn't troubled to see his daughter off. Had she even got on the train to Montréal? What could've happened? Silently cussing to himself that he hadn't thought of it in the first place, he knew Sparks would have to be asked precisely that.

He also decided he had time to go to the train station before meeting up with Davies and, after a nod of thanks to the clerk, started off in that direction.

He was feeling out of sorts from the day's events and thought the walk would help.

He had expected to feel some kind of excitement, some pride in bringing a few pieces to the puzzle. Instead, he felt depressed, dismayed, mostly from his morning encounters, but also because he hadn't been able to learn more. And anger, he felt anger, simply at the waste of a beautiful young woman's life.

*Damn this murdering madman to hell.*

Donahue walked purposefully through the sticky downtown streets, his thoughts still percolating. *Who cares about this young woman anyway? I didn't know her, I'm not responsible for her. Why am I caring like this?*

Which is about when he realized… Davies cared, too.

CHAPTER 20.

Stepping out of the morgue, it was beginning to sink in for Davies that his early-morning reprieve had been just that -- a reprieve and, by definition, only temporary.

He was unconsciously grinding his teeth again, clenching his fists, and that old nagging anxiety was back. Chastising his weakness, he took one more stab at shaking off the cravings but knew it was a losing battle. He was going to need another taste of hashish.

With a sense of defeat, yet still damning the monkey of his own creation, he slipped around the side of the building to find a quiet spot.

Within moments, and with closed eyes, he blew out the smoke – waiting to be free, mind and body. Finally calming, he stubbed out and stuck the butt-end in his tin. Now he was ready for Doolan's.

Looking up as he turned to exit the alley, Davies was confronted by the round figure of Joe Levy, grinning a sweaty grin. He was leaning against a wall at the entrance, wiping his forehead with his sleeve.

"Fancy meeting you here."

"How's it you appear out of nowhere, a man of your size, and just happen to be waiting for me at the moment I might know something."

"It's a gift," Levy said, taking a step into the alley. "Ooh, you look like hell. You been making friends again?"

"You know me, nothing but friendly."

"You find out anything interesting in there?"

"Didn't ya hear? It's the Ripper."

Levy looked at Davies with a withering disappointment and shook his head.

"Ya know, the day before your girl here was found, twenty-eight people died in this heat wave. That's a huge story. This city's never seen temperatures like it. Now this Ripper madness, a prominent suicide and a person gunned down in the street - in broad daylight. People are starting to think it's the end of the world or something. This 'Ripper' story, Ifan, is wiping everything else off the front page. So, I'm asking, are you on to something."

"Not sure yet, Joe. Listen, I promise you, when I do have something solid, you're at the top of my list."

Davies pushed past the newsman when a thought popped in and turned back.

"You happen to know anything about Franklin Ashfield?"

"The MP?"

"That's the guy."

"Not much but I'm sure I could find out."

"Good, talk soon."

Now, anxious that he'd lost time, he was on the move again. He needed to have a few more words with Mickey, fearing he'd do something rash, so stepped up his pace. He heard from behind him…

"Sorry to hear about Little Sean!"

Davies was glad to be free again. The walk would also give him some much-needed time to think, time to sort out the many pieces muddling up his thoughts he was trying to put together.

The entire city was becoming gripped in either fear or excitement -probably both -- and the newspapers are wetting themselves waiting for another barbarous attack. Just as profitable as those phony white slavery ring stories, maybe even more. What the press didn't know was that the murderer had probably already struck again. But who was going to notice somebody like Little Sean?

Suddenly, Ifan was at the front of Doolan's. For a moment, he thought about finishing off that ciggy-butt but took a pass and headed down the steps.

Doolan, standing over a table where two of his boys were killing time, looked up at the sound of the door.

"Christ, now that you've come back to the world, I can't shake your ugly fookin' face."

Ifan nodded a smile and made his way to the bar, slapped down a coin and, on sudden impulse, heard himself order a stout. It had been days now, but this somehow seemed, if not smart, then at least okay. Just a beer.

The place was otherwise empty and Doolan's guys were no longer concerned about his presence. Hadn't been, no doubt, since they'd heard Mickey had urinated on his head. Now, he was serving him a beer.

"Thanks Mickey, I'm gonna appreciate this," said Ifan, cradling the glass but not yet ready to drink. "Just wondering, you hear anything more on Sean?"

"Same as what I told you yesterday."

"Listen Mickey, that's why I'm here. I know you're looking to find who killed Sean. I know *you* want to kill the scum."

"And what if I was?"

"Well, that's the thing. I need information from whoever it is. I want to talk to him before he… before you…"

"Ya, I know. You want to know who his boss is."

"That's right."

"Well, one, why aren't you supposin' I want to know who's paying him as much as you do? And two, Ifan, why would I help you?"

As if by instinct, the two men abruptly stopped speaking when the door to the bar opened and, the back-lit silhouette of Donahue appeared. Walking in, Donahue stopped a few steps short of the bar fearing he was intruding, something Davies waved off with a convivial manner.

"How 'bout another stout for another hard-workin' copper, eh, Mickey? What ya think Jimmy?"

Donahue was dumbfounded, speechless. He knew Davies' reputation for drink - hadn't really thought about till that moment – but he hadn't seen him take so much as a sip over the last few days. Seeing the untouched beer in front of Davies and Doolan's expectant face, Donahue felt compelled to be one of the boys. And appreciated as that was though, all he could muster in response was,

"Okay, I guess."

When Donahue's glass arrived, Davies raised his towards him, gave him a wink and the two took a quaff, while Doolan took a moment to converse with his lads.

Davies quickly turned to Donahue and lowered his voice.

"Anything from the steam ship line?"

"The Sparks girl, she never got on the boat. Also, I had time to check in at the train station."

"And?" Davies inquired, giving Donahue an approving side glance.

"Not a thing, the ticket office couldn't recollect seeing her, as it was a crush of passengers that day and the same went for the taxicab stands."

"A shame. Well, good work son."

Davies took another gulp, this one deeper than his first, as Doolan returned.

"Now, I know you two sorta met but… Jimmy, this is Mickey Doolan, an old friend. Mickey, this is constable Jimmy Donahue. He's a good one."

Doolan and Donahue nodded quietly to one another, and Davies continued on.

"Mickey and me, we'd just been reminiscing about our friend, Sean, when you walked in. He's the one shot to death up the street here yesterday."

"I'm aware. Sorry."

"Actually," Doolan chipped in, "your inspector friend here had dropped by to caution me about getting a little over-anxious. You know, helping you do your jobs."

Donahue, unsure where this conversation might be headed, shot a quizzical look at Davies, who decided he might try to clarify.

"Naw, Mickey, I was just trying to tell you that, if your eyes and ears out there uncover something or someone, I'd hope you'd get in touch with me first before you take… ah, an irrevocable action."

"Well, you could argue my entire life has been an irrevocable action."

"Yes, circumstances have determined a path for you, but I'm asking you to consider taking a different path this time."

"I do love these little heart-to-heart chats we been havin' of late, Ifan, but it may be hard to control the passions of my people, -- if you get my fookin' meanin'."

Doolan's brogue had a habit of becoming thicker when he was menacing people.

"I do, I do. But you think it over, Mickey." said Davies, downing what was left of his stout and grimaced. "Gawd, that's a harsh pint, Mickey."

"I'll be sure to stock up on my genteel beverages for the next time you're in."

With a nod to their host, the two coppers got up to leave, Doolan's gaze following them out the door.

On the street, Davies quickly put a cigarette together, then went looking for a match. Donahue, the perennial boy-scout, had a loose one in his pocket and promptly brought it sizzling to life with a flick of his thumb nail.

"Nice trick," Davies noted.

"Sir, if I may?"

"What's that?"

"Exactly what was going on in there?"

"Ya, not sure that was a good plan." Davies said, rubbing the back of his head and neck. "Hoping, I suppose."

"For what, sir?"

"Hoping history will persuade. Sentiment that is… planting seeds, Donahue."

"I'm not sure I understand, sir."

"No matter, son." Davies said, giving Donahue a light shove to start him moving along.

As they began to walk, Davies was already adrift in thought. They would have to talk to the family again and that was going to be…

"Donahue, since you've already been to the train station and made inquiries, I need you to interview the Sparks family again. They know you and I need for you to follow up and ask if there's a photograph of her? They didn't bring one to the station when they filed the report."

"Yes sir, and then?"

Davies knew Donahue could use a little direction, but he was still badly distracted, now shifting his focus to his own mountain of resurfacing self-doubt.

He was feeling old and stupid again. In this time with Doolan, he couldn't point to a moment or a word but still had this horrible sense that he'd been acting foolishly, arrogantly. There'd been something ridiculous about his play with Mickey, an uncomfortable realization that the past is just that, the past.

"Sir?... What then?"

Donahue was still there.

"Ah, the Sparks, okay? Let's see how long that takes you. If you find anything or need me, send a message to my rooms, not division."

And, with that, Davies stepped into the late-afternoon foot-traffic heading north.

Donahue watched uneasily for a moment, the shadow of worry passing, then pulled out his notebook to be sure he'd taken down the Sparks' address. He could be there before they sat down for supper.

CHAPTER 21.

What Ifan hadn't fully understood, until the moment Doolan cautioned him that it might be hard to control "the passions of my people," was that he was no longer one of those people.

Certainly not one of Doolan's people - since he and Mickey had had that long ago falling out - but a person from the Ward, born and raised.

He had long felt – maybe always felt - that, no matter what, even becoming a copper, he was from the Ward. There was some unspoken bond that, if you came from the Ward, you were always, as the Yids would say, Mishpachah (Family)

He realized now that he'd been cast out of that past and didn't matter to that world anymore. He was a man without a home. They had cut him dead and, these many years later, it had taken him by surprise.

He had made another mistake, too, and he could feel it rumbling in his gut, pricking at his soul, as he licked and savored the remnants of stout on his lips.

The devil was back, and it only took a few sips.

Shaking himself into the present, Ifan turned onto Elizabeth and headed north into the heart of the Ward.

He'd been worried about King Sol, whom he hadn't seen since the late evening of the day the murder had been discovered. *Had someone noticed the King seeing Sean coming out of that alley? Or seen*

*him talking with him? Could Sean's fate now be await-
ing Sol?*

*And who would even care? About a small-time
hoodlum like Sean? Nobody.  An old Jewish rag-
man/peddler? Less than nobody. If I put that old man
in harms-way, I'll never forgive myself.* Davies already
scanning whatever alleys he passed, was headed towards Trinity Square near the ever-growing Eaton's
warehouses.  The scavenging was usually pretty good
there, lots of bits of fabric, odds and ends.

Ifan's heart calmed when his hunch proved correct. The King was there at Trinity, his cart almost full
as he stood to arch and stretch his back. The old man
saw him coming, scratched his motley grey beard and
smiled with his wry weary eyes.

"Boychick, I was beginning to think you was lost."

"You won't get rid of me that easy, kid."

"Kid! That's a good one. So, what brings you
around this time?"

"I'm sure you heard about Little Sean?"

"Oy, what a mess. Not a good business. And in
broad daylight like that."

"You know why I'm looking for you then. I just
wanted to make sure you were okay."

"Sure, sure I'm okay. What else?"

"You hear or see anything regarding Sean's murder? Anything? This guy came out of nowhere, even Mickey Doolan hasn't found out boo. I mean nothing. If he had, the guy would be dead already."

Davies could hear the old man's stomach start to growl, and knew he was thinking about his dinner as he listened to him, while pacing agitatedly from curb to curb.

"Sorry, I don't know what to tell ya. I've heard nothing, seen nothing. Maybe Mama can help you out?"

"Why Mama?"

"I hear she had some nasty business a few weeks ago and Sean had to bounce some rich kid from her joint. Some kinda hubbub with another rich gent."

"Anything else?"

"Whad'ya mean, anything else?"

"You hear if any of those two threatened him?"

"No. No Sean was talking nicely to them. You should talk to Mama."

"I think I'll do that," said Ifan, tenderly putting a hand on his old friend's back. With a grunt, the King readied to put his cart into motion.

"You be careful, boychick."

"Not much fun that way."

"All the same, huh?" The old man said over his shoulder.

Ifan watched the King make his way, weary and stooped over the cart full of his life. He admired the fortitude but hated the oppressive circumstances that created it and, as he often did, walked away feeling helpless and angry.

CHAPTER 22.

Ifan figured it had been months without his dropping in on Mama but now, for the second night in three,
here he was again.

This part of the Ward he knew especially well.
Mama's place, above the laundry of course. He, more
or less, grew up there. That particular doorway just up
the alley, that was where he and Hèlene had talked of
dreams.

He was transfixed on that doorway just now, having taken a few moments to revisit the dog-end he'd
started up hours ago outside the morgue. *Just to take
the edge off.* Two quick puffs and he was good. And
memories, as always, quickly flooded in.

*

"So, you say you want to take me away from all
this. How are we going to live? Where are we going to
live? And do you think Mama is just going to let me walk
out the door?"

The young woman with blue eyes and raven hair
had put her leg up on a chair next to the washstand
and, with a piece of old flannel began to wipe away the
afternoon's fucking.

"Ya, that's what I say, Hèlene. I don't want to be
locked up in this shit-hole the rest of my life."

Ifan rolled over on the bed looking for a cigarette
in his jacket pocket that, along with everything else

he'd been wearing, had been strewn to the floor in the haste of youth.

"That's nice of you to say so, but that ain't reality."

"Hèlene, I'm making plans."

Head propped up with a pillow, he lit his smoke and lay splayed across the sheets in all his glory. She looked at him as she dried herself, thinking she wished it were true.

He inhaled, held the cigarette out to her, then had to smile as she took it in her slender hand. There was just a beautiful toughness, an unromantic way she placed a cigarette between her lips. She began to dress, squinting, the smoke stinging her eyes.

*

"Damn it!", he said out loud, trying to shake away the memory, only to fall right back into another, as if to finish this chapter. His self-doubts about being a copper and why he kept doing it.

So why had he wanted to become a cop? Was he looking for some measure of authority, some power, or did it represent the sheer antithesis to what he was that drew him to it?

Maybe it was a need to destroy the past, to obliterate who he once was and the small, foolish dreams he had held as a teenager. Maybe he did it for her.

Maybe it didn't matter.

The hurt, though, would never leave him. Just as eventually, turning his back on the Ward created a hurt they'd never let him forget. The path he chose made him an outlier, a traitor, to the code of the street. He would always be suspect. He could never go home.

Instead, he pushed himself off the wall he'd been leaning on, crossed the street and headed up the stairs to Mama's.

"Well, look who's suddenly a regular again," she said as Ifan was being given the once-over by one of Mama's young doormen. Ifan could see himself at that age in the kid -- stern, no sense of humour and most likely violent.

"He's alright, honey," she assured her man, dismissing him with a wave of her hand, offering Ifan a seat next to her --for the price of a kiss on the cheek.

"I'm guessing you still haven't found who killed that young woman."

"You'd be guessing right."

The two took each other in for a quiet moment or two, each with a slight smile, with the knowledge of a shared pain.

"Little Sean, huh," Mama finally broaching the unsaid.

"Ya, Sean. It was terrible, Mama. I can still see it."

"He was a good kid, like you."

"I'm also hearing he had a run-in with some swells a few weeks back."

"He did."

"You wouldn't happen to know the names of these gents now, would you?"

"You see *that* question puts me in a difficult position, Ifan. You know my clients come to me because of my discretion. If I break their confidence, I'm out of business or worse."

"I've got a hunch that, in the future, you might not have any business."

Mama sat back in her chair, lit herself a cigar. She could see Ifan wasn't in the mood for play and, taking a long haul, while she weighed her thoughts.

"Well, I'm not sure what I can tell you."

"I know how you operate, Mama. Nobody comes under your roof who you don't know something about."

The big lady leaned even farther back on her throne, took another long pull, and waited.

Ifan always had the feeling that, when Mama sat back like that, smoking, saying little, looking at you through half-closed eyes, occasionally nodding, you were about to walk into something. What that something was you never knew until it was too late.

That's the way Mama liked to play it. You'd get this uncomfortable feeling of falling out of control. You'd simply start babbling, giving up everything, until that moment you realize you were the only one talking.

Ifan smiled, nodding his recognition of the situation he was about to put himself into.

"Do you recall the name of the rich kid Sean bounced a few weeks ago?"

"You know this could fuck me, right?"

"If I can keep your name out of this, you know I will."

"Uh huh," said Mama, spitting out a piece of tobacco that was stuck to her tongue. "Well, hell, even if you do, they'll know it's me."

"Maybe. But listen, Mama, I think there's a connection here to the person who killed Sean and the young woman. Word has dried up on the street. Nobody knows who killed Sean or why. I've got hunches but I've got nothin' connecting any dots for me."

Ifan was being careful not to hard-sell the "Little" Sean sentiment. It was a harsh life in the Ward. People died and sentiment wouldn't go very far, especially coming from him.

"I knew the kid. He'd been comin' around a lot. Spendin,' drinkin,' he was kinda wild. That night, some other gent crashes his party, calling him a no good, dirty Jew whoremongering so and so. The kid goes crazy. Wants to kill the gent. That's when Sean gets between them, breaks it up."

"You know the name of this kid?"

"Alexander Miller."

"No shit?"

"No shit. Sean got him outta here, then starts cooling down the gent and they wind up having a nice long conversation."

"You know his name?"

"Nah."

Ifan knew she was lying to him but decided not to press her.

He rubbed his tired eyes the day starting to catch up with him. This must've been apparent to Mama, and she leaned in to comfort him.

"I'm sure something'll come. Don't beat up on yourself. You been helping yourself out like I told you? You been layin' off the booze?"

"Yes, Mama. I was just hoping… never mind, it's okay. Alexander Miller that was interesting and thanks for that. But let me ask, is there anything else, anything you might've overheard? What did Sean tell you after the gent had left?

Mama sat back and was silent again. She appeared to be chewing on a thought, wrestling with how to say what she didn't want to say.

"Ashfield."

"Ashfield what?"

"The rich guy. The kid knew him, said his name, Ashfield. I remember the Miller kid trying to take a swing at him and said something like, 'You can take your high and mighty Ashfield name and shove it up your ass,' or something like that. It made me laugh. That's why I remember it."

"Hmm, that's some specific detail." Ifan said, taking a sharper look at Mama. "And he had a long talk with Sean, ya?"

"Long talk. Half-hour maybe."

"And, Mama, when you mentioned 'high and mighty' there, that Ashfield gent, he kinda sounds a bit posh, huh?"

"Oh ya, very."

Ifan stopped the questioning for a moment, looked at Mama clearly and gave her a melancholic smile. Suddenly he was the farthest thing from tired. He was revitalized, almost overwhelmed with excitement. He had come hoping for something to nudge things along...

Like he'd always thought, with Mama, you never knew what you were walking into. He bounced out of his chair and gave Mama a huge kiss on the lips.

"Mama, thank you, but I gotta go."

"Go on, get."

Ifan needed air. He wanted to be on the street, to be walking in the night. With a cigarette, God love it. To rethink his puzzle. He could almost hear the pieces clicking together.

CHAPTER 23.

The sun was long-gone as Davies stepped back into the street, but the heat and humidity wore on.

Another sleepless night was in store and not just because of the weather. Davies' mind was alight with activity and excitement. He could sense the whole picture coming together.

*Why was Ashfield at Mama's? She said, he had "crashed" Miller's party. Was he stalking him? Looking for some reason, some evidence against him, to convince his sister that Miller was no good? Was Ashfield a patron?*

He immediately regretted not having asked Mama that and considered going back. But she'd always been guarded when he mentioned her clientele, what made him think she'd be more forthcoming now?

No, what was most important, was the fact that Ashfield, Miller and, specifically, Sean, had a run-in only a week or so before the events of Miller's suicide and the murdered girl.

Davies began to think it would be a good idea to speak with Miss Ashfield again. His instinct was telling him there was more to her grief than the sudden loss of her fiancé.

But how was that going to happen? McCloud had made it clear that there would be political and professional hell to pay if he tried to interview her again. And even if her brother consented to a meeting, there was no way he'd leave them alone.

Then there was Alexander Miller, who was becoming quite a conundrum. He was distraught and crazed, then committed suicide the morning the body was found. He spoke with a slight accent and had lived in England at the time of the White Chapel murders. Those murders must have left a deep and disturbing mark on the young boy.

To the outside world, he was the son of a rich and successful man and moving up in his own right in the realm of finance. To Katherine Ashfield, he was a poet and her fiancé, while her brother considered him a dirty Jew, was not worthy of his sister. Mama knew him for his more carnal needs. And the father? Did he know his son at all?

There were ties between all these events and Sean was right in the middle of it all and never knew.

Davies was teasing out these thoughts as he stepped off the curb, oblivious to the loud clattering of hooves and wheels screaming directly at him. He looked up just in time to catch a glimpse of the masked driver, but had it not been for the shouts and furious gestures from a newsboy who was hawking his last few papers of the day he'd most likely be dead.

At the last possible moment, he dove back across the sidewalk, getting to an elbow in time to see it, the hurtling wagon, still at full-roar, disappear around the next corner.

The newsboy and a couple of passers-by were quick to his side and helped him to his feet. All agreed there'd been no cry of warning from the driver. There was an elderly gent who offered that he'd felt the wagon had been slowly tailing Davies, by maybe forty yards, for a couple of blocks, the horses lashed into top speed only when it became apparent a distracted Davies was about to step into the street. He understood immediately it had been no accident.

He took a wary glance about the street, gave the newsie the few coins he had, asked for one of the papers and continued home.

Notwithstanding his regular bouts with self-doubt, Davies felt he'd been working as quickly and efficiently as he had in years but now he knew he'd have to re-double his efforts. Someone was getting very nervous out there and wanted his investigation stopped. Clearly, he was making progress, but he was also an obvious, if not only, target.

*

When he got within a half-block of his bedsit, Davies noticed a carriage out front and knew whatever it was, it had to do with him. Coming to a dead stop for a moment, the thought of a bullet to the head crossing his mind, he made his way cautiously forward, breathing a sigh of relief when he saw the driver on the sidewalk adjusting the horse's harness. When the driver noticed Davies, he stepped to the carriage and said something in the window. A second later, a head popped out.

"Inspector Davies, is that you?"

It was John Miller.

"Well, this is a surprise," said Davies, in utter honesty, as he strode up alongside the carriage.

"Not to worry, I won't ask to come in. But please join me here. There are a few things I need to get straight."

The two sat across from one another in the half dark of the carriage, illuminated only by the gaslight from the street. Miller sat well back in his seat and Davies couldn't actually see him but for an outline. The whole scene had a very confessional atmosphere about it. Very intimate.

He waited, listening to Miller's breathing in the silence, sensing the conflicted emotions of the man.

"You've never had a son, have you inspector?" Miller began, slowly feeling his way.

"No." Davies replied, prepared to allow the man whatever time he needed to unburden himself, for that, it turned out, was exactly what he had come here to do.

"I have to tell you first, our last argument, my son's and mine, wasn't about his engagement."

"What was it about then?"

He only wished he could see Miller's face to get a handle on what was truly going on inside the man.

"Do you know what it is to have a son who's a miscreant? I'm sorry, of course you don't. Well, I'll tell you, it rips your heart out."

"Why are you telling me this?"

"Maybe I need to be absolved."

"By a stranger? Where do I come into this?"

"I have no doubt you've already found out some things about Alexander. Perhaps I need you to keep them quiet."

"Things like what?"

"Alexander was a spoiled child and an even greater spoiled adult. It's perhaps my fault, or money and the lack of true responsibility."

"And?"

"I see you don't have much sympathy for spoiled rich children."

"You'd be correct, sir."

"Fair enough. As much as I wanted him to take responsibility it always ended up that I was indulging his lack of responsibility. I paid his debts. I turned my head to his appetites and indiscretions. I always hoped that, someday, he would grow out of it all. But he didn't and, in fact, his debauched life accelerated, culminating in his absurd belief that he would marry the Ashfield girl."

"Absurd how? They were of an age and of the same social status and, by her account, in love."

"Ha, in love," said Miller, brushing off the idea with a dismissive and bitter chuckle, then shifting forward in his seat.

"The night we argued, Alexander came to me, once again asking for money. He had gambling debts and owed money all over town for any number of illegal… proclivities. He begged me, told me he was going to change, that Katherine had made a new man of him."

"But, for the first time, I refused him and what followed were many bitter recriminations replete with accusations and threats. Finally, I struck a blow I'm ashamed of, something I said designed to hurt. It was something he could never run from, something intended to end his ideas of marriage and his free lifestyle."

Miller broke off, turning away to look out the window. He pondered his shame, avoiding Davies eyes that he imagined were adjusting to the dimly lit carriage, staring at him in judgement.

"I reminded him he was a Jew and, therefore, would always be on the outside, hated. Franklin Ashfield would never allow the marriage, and, without money, I doubted she would follow him and his foolish ideas of being a poet. I made him see the romantic illusion was only that, a fantasy. A woman as well-bred as Miss Ashfield wasn't going to throw it all away and live in poverty. Living in a garret would weary quickly."

"I just wasn't going to help him out anymore. I was done picking up for him and paying for his messes. When he left that day, he was calm. I believed that he had accepted the truth of his situation, and, with time, we would move on. As you know, I was very wrong."

Davies listened intently to the confession in the dark, looking for another thread he could follow to his killer. Unfortunately, as Miller said at the onset, he was looking for absolution, for someone to tell him that he wasn't a bad father.

As he tried to frame some kind of response, Davies had to wonder why Miller would even care what he thought.

"What you don't know, sir, is that Alexander had a run-in with Franklin Ashfield only a short time ago. I fear you only reinforced his self-loathing and that his idea of a marriage to Katherine was ridiculous and ill conceived. I'm sorry, but I do thank you for what you've told me."

What Davies had stopped short of saying was that the father had shattered his son's last possible hope, that all Alexander's dreams and plans were only an illusion of the desperate.

Stepping down from the carriage, Davies could just make out the features of Miller's face. The man was still in pain and whatever he had come to let go of hadn't occurred.

Miller tapped the roof of the cabin with his walking stick, signaling the driver to move on, then turned to stare out the opposite window as the carriage headed down the empty street.

CHAPTER 24.

Finally, back in his room, Ifan stripped down to his boxer shorts, draping his jacket and trousers over his one simple chair. He hung his shirt in the window to air and dry, then ran a rag over the dust on his boots.

He did all this trying not to think about the one thing he really wanted. *Maybe because more and more memories and dreams of Hélene kept coming up these days.* He thought.

*To hell with it. Why not?*

Reaching behind his headboard, Ifan's outstretched fingers felt for the bottle he'd stashed in case of an emergency. It didn't take much to convince himself that almost getting killed in the street constituted one of those. Not only that, but things were also going well. He deserved a little celebration.

Davies held up the bottle, examining how much he had left. "That'll do," he said to the empty room. He pulled the cork, raised the bottle to his lips. The burn was not just in his throat but deep in his chest, or deeper still, a scraping at his soul.

As always, the first sips of whisky brought comfort, then a feeling of joy and satisfaction for the success he'd had over the last few days. A few more sips, though, and a sense of guilt and sadness wormed its way in. By morning it would be just plain disgust.

He laid down on the bed, staring blankly at the ceiling's peeling paint and old water stains. Licking his thumb and forefinger he reached for the candle and pinched out the flame. The outside air was still, and for another night, the open window would be bringing no relief. The thought of crawling under his sheets made him irritable, so he lay on top, even though he knew he'd be shivering in the morning.

He also knew the only cure for his mounting disgust was one more drink. He reached for the bottle and drained the dregs, wincing at the burn, then rolled the empty under his bed. If not a cure, he could at least pass out. But it wouldn't keep the dreams at bay.

*

Hèlene was always talking about wanting to go to school. For what, she wasn't sure. She'd say she'd figure it out when she got there. She always had to laugh, always teased him about his plan to join the constabulary.

"Why you wanna go become a copper?"

"I dunno, I just do. It's gotta be better than living like this."

In the end, the dreams didn't much matter.

That winter would be hard weather, and a brutal influenza swept the Ward. Many got sick, many died. Neither Ifan nor Hélene were aware how bad it was until she took ill. He would never forget those long sick days and nights watching her slowly leave him, his worst fears finally realized in a shaking, coughing pool of sweat.

It was a cruel death. They were both in the prime of youth, both bursting into one another. She, so beautiful, so full of life; he, for all his strength, left with nothing he could do. It was the only love he had ever known, and the pain of its loss was unbearable. It broke him.

*

Finally, back in his room Donahue took off his tunic and trousers, setting them in their usual spot on his poor man's valet. He lay down on the bed, propped up by his pillow, in his shirt and underwear, exhausted from the day.

He'd had been late getting to the Sparks, who'd already gone out for the evening. He felt like he'd let the inspector down somehow. Tomorrow he'd be there early.

Donahue's eyelids were becoming heavy, the day leaving him for the dreams of his future where he'd give free rein to his fantasies, desires, and ego. Elevated to full-fledged inspector, he'd become another of those working-class heroes. But he would really do things. He wouldn't squander the opportunity like others before him. He could make a difference.

He reached for the lamp. In the dark, ambition filled his thoughts as sleep finally took him away.

CHAPTER 25.

Following another of his regular briefings at the mayor's office, with both the Chief and the Mayor, McCloud strode into division well after the morning shift change. These sessions were always lengthy and never pleasant, but he endured them with the sweet knowledge that he'd outlast the career of yet another city leader.

Passing the sergeant's booking desk to a chorus of "morning sirs" from constables readying to hit the streets, McCloud was steps from his office when he pulled to a halt.

"Jesus am I dreaming?" he announced, genuinely dumbfounded. "Do my eyes deceive me? Is this inspector Ifan Davies *actually* sitting at his desk doing the tedious part of police work?"

"Yup, you caught me" said Davies, never looking up as he feverishly applied the finishing touches to a whole series of reports he'd neglected over the past several days.

McCloud made his way over to Davies' desk and casually fingered a few of the pages, not even doing a reasonable job of appearing interested. Davies was in no mood for the distraction McCloud intended to provide. Besides trying to decipher half a notebook of his drunken scrawls, he was also dealing with his first hangover in days.

"Not to worry, almost done. They'll be on your desk in another minute, and you'll have all day to go through them."

"Lucky me. At least, I'll finally have something to say when the mayor drags me back into his office to explain why there's been no arrest and Jack the Ripper is still on every front page."

"You, poor dear."

"Listen Davies, you sent the press howling in that direction," McCloud threatened, leaning in. "This is your mess. I'm only going to give you so much rope. You better give me something concrete soon, no more games."

"Well, these may disappoint but, as of right now, there are few solid conclusions, just a series of facts. Pretty dry reading if you ask me."

"And when do you think you might be able to draw any kind of conclusion, hmm?" McCloud queried.

"Again, not to worry, it's coming."

With that, Davies scooped his pile of reports, straightened them up with a couple of raps on the desk and handed them to McCloud.

"Enjoy," he said and headed for the door, where, in what was becoming a habit of theirs, Davies and Donahue practically crashed into one another.

"Whoa, son! You about killed me with that door."

"Sorry, sir. I was hoping to catch you here. I've just ridden down from Rosedale, from the Sparks' place. I thought I…"

Donahue was excited and nearly out of breath. Davies glanced back to be sure McCloud hadn't noticed them, then took Donahue's elbow, and quickly steered him back outside.

"By the way, I thought I told you to come to my digs, not here?"

"I did. You weren't there. And what's going on anyway?" Donahue snapped back as he was being hustled down the street.

"Okay, listen, someone tried to kill me last night."

"What!" Blurted out a stunned Donahue.

"I'm fine, as you can see, he missed his mark. Someone's watching me. I can't trust anyone just now. Except you. You, kid, I trust."

The off-hand confession triggered a pang of guilt in Donahue. McCloud had ordered him to report back on Davies' every move and he'd done nothing of the sort - never intended to really, even though he knew there'd be hell to pay. How could he ever tell Davies of this now? His partner trusted him. He couldn't think about it now and pushed the thoughts aside.

"So, Jimmy, the Sparks family, then."

"Yes. Inspector, our Jane Doe...she's... I'm pretty sure she's Eugenia Sparks."

"And why are you thinking that?"

"Well, I got both parents, Donald and his wife, Myrtle. It turns out neither had indeed taken Eugenia to the train station. They had sent her luggage on ahead, said their goodbyes at home and Eugenia went to see a friend before she was supposed to catch her train."

Davies was becoming very intrigued. "And she's our Jane Doe because..."

"Because, while I was taking their statements, luckily, I saw a family photo on the piano in their living room and didn't have to request one. I asked if they could point out Eugenia for me. The mother was more than pleased to show it off and, when she handed it to me, I immediately recognized Eugenia to be our young woman. Or at least eighty percent sure. Of course, I never studied the body as intently as you did that day in the alley, but I'm pretty sure."

"Did you bring the photo?"

"I did," Donahue said, pulling the photo from his pocket. "I believe she fits the description.

Davies took the photograph and studied it. But it didn't take long to recognize the smiling face that was staring back at him. Looking back up to Donahue he asked.

"Please tell me you got the name of the friend she went to visit?"

Donahue had been waiting for that and, as a slow smile began to brake across his face, he announced, with a certain measure of pride:

"Katherine Ashfield."

Ifan grinned and nodded to Donahue. "Good job, Jimmy. Let's get the bikes from the garage. This is our way back in."

CHAPTER 26.

Davies gave three sharp raps on the brass knocker then stepped back to await the arrival of the Ashfields' butler.  He and Donahue stood sharing an awkward silence, each contemplating the job they had to do and the possibilities that lay within.

The door jerked open and the butler, as dour as Davies remembered, gave both men a disdainful once-over, then condescended to ask why they were there.

"And good afternoon to you, too, James. I'm sure you remember me. Inspector Davies. This is constable Donahue."

"Miss Katherine is indisposed at the moment and not taking visitors today, sir. Might I suggest you make an appointment through Mr. Ashfield's office for another time."

"You may suggest it, but it's imperative we speak with Miss Ashfield right now."

Davies had advanced up the one step to the entrance and, anticipating the butler's intention to close the door on them, quickly stuck his foot in to block it.

"Now, James, that's not very friendly, is it?"

"As I said, inspector, the lady is not available."

"I really must insist…"

"What the devil's going on here?" boomed an agitated Franklin Ashfield, now making his way to the door.

"Excuse me, sir, but there are some questions I need to ask your sister," said Davies, taking the opportunity to slip past the butler and come face to face, yet again, with Ashfield.

"I don't see what could be so important that it couldn't wait for a proper appointment."

"Murder."

"Murder? What murder? What are you talking about?"

"We believe your sister may know something of the identity of the young woman who was murdered in the Ward."

"Nonsense. It's preposterous that Katherine would ever be associated with, let alone know, some prostitute from the Ward."

"Well, as I told you before, on one of your visits to McCloud's office, we're pretty certain she wasn't a prostitute."

Davies' tone indicated he was deadly serious, in no mood to be dissuaded.

"And who do you think this person, this woman, was?"

"That I will discuss with your sister."

Both men held their ground and Donahue, also now in the entranceway, had no idea how this was going to play out until…

"Very well. James, would you please call for Miss Katherine to join us in the living room. This way, gentlemen."

"I remember, thank you." said Davies, already heading that way, delighting in the knowledge that Ashfield had to be bristling over this reminder that he'd already been in his house.

After Davies declined a seat, Ashfield countered with, "Well, may offer you gentlemen a cigar, then?"

Donahue, awkwardly leaning against the door frame, politely refused in his best 'I'm on duty' manner, while Davies flashed a bright smile. There was nothing he enjoyed more than the rich having to humble themselves, using all the manners they'd been taught, to cover their discomfort around the lower sort.

"Don't mind if I do," he said, selecting a cigar from the box proffered by Ashfield, dragging it under his nose, inhaling the spice. As Ashfield struck a match, Davies bit off the end in a rustic fashion, took the light and savoured.

"Very nice."

"Remind me to send you a box."

"I will."

Donahue could only watch as this pantomime unfolded, not at all sure what he was even doing there. Mercifully, that's when the butler returned, leading a disheveled and not-altogether-present Katherine Ashfield.

"James why are you dragging me down to…oh, you! I know you. You're the inspector. We met, oh, when was that?" Again, she floated into the room, sat herself in the same chair she had previously, then looked past those in the room to a space beyond the window inhabited by dreams.

"As you see, inspector, my sister really isn't up for any interrogation right now. If you'd care to…"

"No, no, we'll be fine," said Davies insinuating Ashfield's departure with a gesture towards the door. "If you don't mind."

Ashfield looked like someone who wasn't quite sure he'd just heard what he'd heard.

"Excuse me? I do think it best, as Katherine's guardian, that I'm present."

"And why is that?"

"To protect her."

"From what?" said Davies, tilting his head, feigning innocent surprise at the notion.

Finding it difficult to answer why his sister needed protecting, Ashfield could only sputter some nonsense about her infirmity and that they had nothing to hide, which Davies easily brushed off.

"If you don't mind, Donahue, would you escort Mr. Ashfield out of the room so I can speak with Miss Ashfield."

Hearing herself referred to, Katherine licked her lips and blinked in such a slow manner, Davies wondered if she hadn't fallen asleep.

Ashfield, flabbergasted and bewildered, felt resigned to the situation, and still sputtering - this time in protest - slowly complied.

When the door clicked closed, Davies turned to Katherine. "A pleasure to see you again, Miss Ashfield. Do you mind if I ask you a few more questions?"

"Be my guest," she said, eyes partially closed, looking absently into the garden and, obviously, under the influence of laudanum. "But I told you everything about Alexander and myself. Why do we have to go on about it?"

"I'm not here about your relationship with Mr. Miller. I'm here because I believe Miss Eugenia Sparks came to visit you recently. Is that true?"

"Oh yes, Ginny. But she'll be in England by now." The thought it, sparking some life into Katherine.

"Is it true you saw her the day she was to depart."

"Yes, she came to say goodbye. We've been friends since we were girls. Our families, you know…" Her thoughts trailed off again, as did her words.

Davies had to pause. He felt helpless in the knowledge that addiction and the avoidance of pain went hand in hand but that you can never outrun it. The trauma is always there. He briefly weighed whether he should continue or not. But only briefly.

"And, Miss Ashfield, your brother Franklin? Was he here that day? Did he see Eugenia?"

"Franklin? Oh, yes. He definitely knew she was dropping by."

"Did he and Eugenia speak?"

"Mmm-hmm."

"Do you happen to remember what they spoke of?"

"Absolutely. Normally, over the years, they'd flirt awfully with each other. That day… no, not at all. Franklin got into such a mood, it about ruined Ginny's goodbye visit."

"What kind of a mood would you say? What brought it about?"

The subject of Eugenia and Franklin's flirtatious relationship revived Katherine. She began to speak with greater momentum and the enthusiasm of one who delights in gossip.

"Well, you see, Franklin had gotten it into his head that he should marry

Ginny. He'd been sweet to her for years. Though, I did get the feeling Franklin was more interested in Ginny's family name, a good alliance you see, rather than her as wife.

"We, Ginny, and I, would talk about that, sometimes have a good laugh. But I knew she wanted no part of it, he, being so much older than her. It wasn't that she led him on but did humour him a bit…the flirting, you know. She hoped, in time, the matter would resolve itself."

"And on the day she visited?"

"I know I had tried several times telling Franklin of the reality of the situation and felt he might have finally understood. That day, though, he practically proposed. He told Ginny something about how, when she got back from England, he thought they should start making definite plans."

"And?"

"Ginny was absolutely startled. So was I. She had to let out a laugh. Practically in his face.

"I don't ever feel sorry for my brother, but I did then. He'd been badly wounded, crushed. The colour drained from his face, he was trembling, then he stormed out of the room. Ginny felt terribly, too, and followed him. I could hear them talking in the hallway. A few minutes later, they came back together. It looked like things had been smoothed over. Franklin even asked Ginny to drop him off at his club on her way to the train station and they'd say their final goodbyes on route."

Ifan wasn't quite expecting what he'd just heard, and it slightly took his breath away.

"So, Miss Sparks left with Mr. Ashfield? That would have been around 10 or 11 in the morning?"

"Indeed, she did. After we toasted her."

Davies leaned in trying to contain the mounting excitement of a hound dog on the scent.

"Toasted?"

"Oh, yes. After Franklin pulled himself together, he went and brought in glasses of wine to toast Ginny's travels."

"What do you mean went and brought in? Wouldn't he have had your butler fetch the wine?"

"No, Franklin took charge of that. We may be rich but we're certainly capable of pouring wine for ourselves, inspector."

Davies ignored Ashfield's defensive tone and, wanting to press forward with a thought that had just come to him, casually asked if she could recall the type of wine they'd had.

"Well, Champagne would have been more appropriate, but Franklin insisted on a ridiculously heavy red wine. Poor Ginny. She started to feel tired, a bit light-headed, after our toast. Honestly, Franklin should've known better to serve such a rich wine. And at that hour!"

"Yes, he should have," said Davies, sitting back in his chair to think for a moment, then asking: "Is that when Mr. Ashfield asked to share a ride?"

"It was, yes."

"Did he call for the cab, or was it the one Miss Sparks had arrived in?"

"I'm not sure."

Davies thanked her for her time and stood to leave as Ashfield rested her head against the back of her chair, slipped into a haze and mumbled something to herself he couldn't quite make out.

"Excuse me, miss?"

"I killed him."

"What!" Davies said, stopped in his tracks.

"Alexander. I killed him."

"And how would you have done that?"

To no one in particular, a confession to the room, her eyelids growing heavy, Ashfield spoke in a raspy whisper.

"I was to meet him at City Hall. We were going to elope. I didn't show up. I was too afraid of them and, it broke him, I …I…"

"Them?"

"Alexander knew what they are, how cruel they could be."

"Who's that?"

"Franklin and his society. My lovely boy, he knew all about them, how powerful they are." Closing her eyes, her thoughts trailed off again.

He knew, in her state, any further questions would be futile.

Davies stepped into the foyer and motioned to Donahue, standing sentry, to follow him out. Franklin Ashfield, who'd been seated opposite the living room, jumped to his feet expecting some sort of remark, but was left dumfounded and speechless until the two men almost out the front door.

"Is that it then?" Ashfield yelled after them.

"Yes, that's it," Davies called back over his shoulder. Then, stopping in his tracks, Donahue past through the door, turned to face Ashfield. "One question. What's the name of your club?"

"The Harbinger gentleman's club. Why?"

"Oh, wondering if they're looking for new members."

Ashfield almost took the enquiry seriously and was about to respond, then just as quickly withdrew coldly, and responded with a curt, "you?"

"Probably not, huh?" and with that Davies turned on his heels to re-join Donahue.

"Thank you, Mr. Ashfield. I'm sure we'll be speaking with you very soon."

CHAPTER 27.

Donahue had never seen the inspector like this. Granted he hadn't known him that long at all, but he now looked a far cry from the man he'd roused from a flophouse just four days ago. This was a man who'd had a fire lit beneath him, a determined man with purpose of being - that spark that fuels and drives people.

Whatever it was, Donahue wanted in. It was electric and, as he'd tell people for many years afterward, *you just knew something was going to happen.*

Leaving the Ashfield's home, Davies scrambled for his bicycle and wheeled down the walkway to the street. Once there, instead of turning the way that would've headed them back towards division, he veered left with Donahue in tow, farther into the Rosedale neighborhood. Donahue had cycled that very way only a couple of hours earlier.

"We're going to the Sparks' house, sir?"

"That we are, Jimmy."

"Understood, sir. And if you don't mind me asking, you haven't mentioned how it went at the Ashfield's. I know her brother wasn't pleased. Did Miss Ashfield prove helpful?"

"Very helpful, Jimmy. Very helpful."

They rode hard for two, three minutes, through lush and well-moneyed surroundings, before turning into a small side street and making their way to a three-storey, red brick house on a large corner lot.

Surrounded by a six-foot hedgerow, it might've been an attractive and bright home but was burdened with the drab lifeless functionality of the Presbyterian life so often synonymous with many parts of the city.

Propping their bikes up against the hedgerow, the two took the few steps to the front door. Davies was poised to knock when a jolt of reality stopped him cold.

He'd been lost in the excitement of the hunt and now came to the sudden realization that he was about to tell parents - people he had never met - that their child had been murdered.

He turned towards Donahue with the look of a man searching for some assurance that this, indeed, was what he was supposed to do, would have to do. Donahue's almost imperceptible nod provided it. "Jimmy, would you mind introducing me here? Suddenly. I'm not sure what to say."

Donahue stepped forward and knocked.

There'd be no butler coming to the door at this house. Though wealthy enough, the Sparks employed no household staff other than a cook to help in the kitchen and, on occasion, a local carriage driver who serviced several of the homes in the neighborhood. They hadn't come from money and lived an austere life that bordered on spartan.

The door opened just wide enough for Myrtle Sparks to peep timidly around the frame, her eyes blinking like a mole emerging into the light of day.

"Why hello, constable. We weren't expecting you. Oh, I do hope you have some news of our Eugenia. Have you been able to locate her?"

"Not yet, Mrs. Sparks," he lied. "This is inspector Davies, ma'am. He has a few questions for you. May we come in?"

"Yes, please. Just wait in here. I'll get Mr. Sparks."

She'd directed them to a simply decorated living room, but for a baby grand off the entranceway. Sheer curtains were drawn across the windows, dulling the early afternoon sun that could do little to enliven the modest furnishings. There was virtually no sound throughout and both Davies and Donahue were made to feel that any movement -- even a breath -- was an intrusion. They wondered if people lived there at all.

Donahue, who had come to understand Donald Sparks couldn't help but bellow everywhere he went -- not necessarily to be heard, just to be dominating -- noted that the normal bluster was now being held in check.

"Good day again, sir. This is inspector Davies. I've told him of your daughter's case."

"It's a case now, is it? What does that mean?"

"Well, yes sir," Donahue started to explain, "Once you…"

"Yes, yes, I understand, sorry. So, inspector?"

Davies managed to get in the words "Yes, I…," when Donahue stepped in to provide one more helpful nudge, this one directed more towards Mrs. Sparks.

"The inspector wanted to speak to you about the photograph of your daughter, you'd given me this morning."

"Oh yes, of course," she said, beaming with a mother's pride, "It was taken only a few months ago. Very recent it is, very recent."

Davies thanked her kindly, self-consciously fingering the photo he'd pulled from his coat, his mind racing in anticipation of the speaking the unthinkable.

Then he realized you can't know such a thing in a moment. For all the mistakes he had made in his life, he knew this couldn't be another. He took to studying the photograph again, a detail from the image struck him. And there was no mistake.

Davies glanced up at this proud mother, sickened that, in the next few moments, he was going to break her heart. Shatter her life. But he wasn't yet ready. He needed a stall.

So, he asked if their daughter might've purchased a new wardrobe for her trip to England, one that might have included new Italian shoes?

"Why, yes, she had," said Myrtle. "The shoes, too. How clever."

"Ha! What young woman travelling to Europe for the first time alone wouldn't have a new wardrobe," her husband retorted, dismissing the obvious and insignificant line of questioning. But he was now growing increasingly wary of some terrible inevitability.

"Just wanted to be sure of something," said Davies gently, still trying to find his way.

Donahue had long steeled himself for the unavoidable moment and stood staring at the floor, jaw clenched, hands clasped together behind his back.

The mother, sensing a shift in her visitors' countenances, their uncomfortable behavior, spoke up.

"Make sure of what?" she said, the full dread of her worst thoughts slowly becoming apparent in the treble of her voice.

Davies had no place left to go. "I'm sorry to bring you such news but I believe your daughter is the young woman we found dead in the Ward a few days ago. Mr. Sparks, I will need you to come down to the morgue and identify the body."

Spoken aloud, the statement stunned the room, Davies included. The parents, barely comprehending what they'd just heard, sank to the settee.

"Our Eugenia? You're certain?" the mother asked, a pleading in her eyes allowing every room for a possible mistake.

"I'm sorry, but yes. And I do need Mr. Sparks for a definitive identification."

"You mean now?"

"If you could. Would you also call yourself a carriage? We traveled here on bicycles. Donahue will wait with you, then accompany you downtown."

"Yes, of course, whatever I must do." He stood, now on the verge of tears, unbelieving.

"I need to ask you one more thing sir, if I may?"

Sparks nodded his consent, put his hand on his wife's shoulder as she gently began to sob, turning her head from the men.

"Did your daughter take your carriage when she left to visit Katherine Ashfield the day she was meant to travel?"

"No, I was using it that day, I had business downtown. We'd sent her luggage on earlier, then hired another cab for her."

"Would you happen to remember the name of the company you hired from?"

"Yes, it's written down in my day-book in my office. Do you mind getting that for the inspector, Myrtle? I'll just get my hat and be right back."

The two helped each other out of the living room in a sad silence that would break the heart of the most hardened.

Davies turned to Donahue.

"Jimmy, I don't know if you've been to the morgue, but I need you to get the old boy there. Then, check if Ashfield was dropped off at his club. The Harbinger for gents, the day Eugenia was supposed to be dropped at the train station. I'll make my way back to the morgue as fast as I can. I'm going to head to the cabbie stables to inquire of the driver who, no doubt, was one of the last people to see Miss Sparks alive."

"Yes, sir." Donahue assured as the Sparks made their way back into the room, he with hat and cane, she with a piece of paper that she handed Davies.

The father would never be the same.

"Constable let's step out to wait at the corner," he said quietly. "My carriage will be there momentarily."

He then turned to his wife, clasped her hands in his. "I'll return as soon as possible. Are you sure you'll be alright?"

She avoided her husband's eyes and nodded silently that she'd be okay.

The men stepped out onto the porch, Davies turning back for a moment to tip his hat to the woman slowly retreating behind the door.

"Ma'am, again, I'm so sorry for this awful news."

She never said a word, an iron will, holding her emotions in check, their vulgarity and baseness not to be seen in a woman of her class.

The door clicked closed and was locked from behind.

CHAPTER 28.

Sparks' carriage, with Donahue's escort, had disappeared from view when Davies pushed off on the next leg of his already long day.

The heat was almost bearable, the cicadas were humming, and his hangover had mercifully disappeared as he headed for the stables of Hazelton Cabs, the company Sparks had used. Something was missing, though, and he knew what it was the moment he noticed the empty bench in an inviting little park.

Certain cigarettes - sometimes only one over an entire day - are simply better than others. And here was a moment to take stock, unscramble his thoughts. He was weary, no question, but in these quiet, pastoral surroundings, he also felt a twinge of melancholy, sadness.

The poor Sparks. It had been some time since he'd had to deliver news like that. And Katherine Ashfield, cachu (shit). He could only imagine how Franklin was grilling her at that moment.

He also had a thought about the treadmill he was on and if he'd ever get off it. But it was fleeting. His time was up.

*

Davies was back up to a full head of steam by the time he got to the stables, a busy and noisy place, more-so because of the shift-change in progress.

There were maybe a dozen drivers bustling about, a smithy hammering at wheel rims and a couple of grooms rotating horses in and out of harness.

Davies weaved about, looking for someone who might be in charge and was about to approach a stout, middle-aged gent when he was distracted by one of the cabbies. This was one of the gruffier looking of these and was conspicuous for his total lack of movement amidst all the activity.

While Davies stood puzzled, the cabbie stared back with a look that combined both perplexity and fear. Then, in a bolt, it hit him. Those eyes! He'd seen them twice before – first, in the split-second before Sean took a bullet in the head; then again, the next night, when a speeding wagon tried to run him over.

"You!" Davies shouted, pointing at the cabbie, who tossed aside the halter he'd been working on and broke for the open doors.

Davies was on the move, too, but a few strides behind, hadn't seen which way his man had turned into the busy traffic.

A moment later, he knew.

First, there were the shouts and screams, the wails of drayman and horses desperate to come to an abrupt stop but failing. Davies, caught in the drag of time, turned toward the unforgettable sight and sound of horse and wagon meeting flesh and bone.

The traffic slowed, the gawkers gawked, some barely able to look but compelled to try and many of those, mouths agape, only through their fingers. Other passers-by wanted to stop but slowly moved on, knowing there was nothing to be done. There were also those who adopted grim stares that indicated they were already prepared to accept the horror of this muted moment of tragedy.

Davies was quick to the spot, identified himself as police to the gathering circle and knelt beside the mangled body that lay face-down, unmoving and bleeding in the dusty street.

Realizing he had little time to consider the man's pain or well-being, Davies rolled him over on his back, placing his head in the crook of his arm. The cabbie groaned, his eyes fluttering at the sun and the dust. Then he started coughing up blood, eyes rolling back in his head. Davies knew he had only minutes, if that, to find out what he could.

"Who are you working for?" Davies demanded, looking urgently into the swollen and blood-shot eyes -- the eyes that gave him away. In return, he saw no regret, no cry for God, just the steady stare of defiance, either at him or oblivion, probably both.

"You're dying. If you fear God or feel anything for the grieving parents of a butchered young woman, absolve your soul now. Who hired you?"

The cabbie continued staring directly into him, a malicious smile forming that clearly said, 'to hell with you.' Davies stared back, then, playing his last card, leaned in, and whispered…

"He doesn't give a damn about you."

There was more blood to cough up, a wheezing in his chest, a gurgling in his throat. Then it all just stopped.

Davies stood, took a kick at the ground, and swore quietly to himself, "now I'm fucked." He heard police whistles, the crowd stirring, murmuring. He looked at the body. There'd be no enlightenment here, just stinking death, cruel and undignified as, no doubt, it would come to most.

He turned to look back towards the stables where the entire workforce had gathered on the street, many of whom were clearly angry, upset and grumbled among themselves. Included was the man he'd been about to approach earlier.

"You, sir," Davies called out. "Police Inspector Davies."

There was an urgency in his voice, almost impatience, that made the man, already stressed by the goings-on, even more on edge. He turned out to be named Smith, a manager and dispatcher.

"The driver. What was his name?"

"LeRoy, sir. James LeRoy."

"Would you have a list of his fares from a week or so back, specifically for those beginning July 5th?"

"In my office, yes. Follow me."

Smith hurried back into the stables and, before Davies was even a few steps inside the doors, was on his way back with a clipboard full of pages through which he was already flipping.

"Here," said Smith, a finger pressed to a name and date. "Is this what you're looking for?"

"LeRoy was the driver for the Sparks?"

"Yes, Donald Sparks. LeRoy had been hired for the whole day but returned very late."

"What do you mean?"

"I was working the late shift that night and LeRoy came in after midnight. He said there'd been a problem with the cab but that he'd got it fixed and cleaned. Also, not to worry since Sparks had paid for the inconvenience as well."

"Did he say specifically what had happened to the cab?"

"No, but he handed over the monies due and I thought no more of it. I had a perfectly cleaned and ready cab."

Davies then flipped a few pages forward, looking for LeRoy's name and whatever fares he might have had in the past four or five days. Finding nothing, he handed the clipboard back distractedly, nodded his thanks and sprinted for his bike. His hope was to catch Sparks and Donahue before they left the morgue. With LeRoy's death, he had lost what he had to believe was the killer's last accomplice. He needed to find some other connections - and quick.

CHAPTER. 29

Donahue was having a smoke in front of the morgue when Davies pulled up. "Was it Sparks' daughter? Is he still here?"

"It was sir. And, yes, that's his carriage there waiting."

"And Ashfield's club?"

"The doorman remembers Ashfield arriving around 11ish and not leaving until late afternoon."

Davies stared down at his feet and, for the second time that day, kicked at the ground wanting to swear a blue streak. After a moment, he looked back to Donahue and asked, "where's Sparks?"

"At the moment he's sitting on the bench outside the coroner's office. He's devastated."

"I'm sure he is and, unfortunately I've got another question for him."

The two hurried inside, slowing their pace as they approached the once imposing figure of Donald Sparks, now shrunken and painfully alone. He'd clasped his head in his hands, alternately rubbing his forehead then temples with his finger-tips. His lips were moving silently, perhaps in prayer, thought Davies; perhaps, rehearsing how to relate the unfathomable to his wife -- without detail.

Sparks looked up with the confusion of a man utterly lost and Davies felt a need to put a hand to his shoulder.

"Again, I'm sorry, Mr. Sparks. And, while I know this is a terribly difficult time, I do need to ask you one more question." "Very well," said Sparks, almost inaudibly.

"The company that picked up your daughter that day tells me the cab had some trouble and had to be fixed and cleaned before it was returned. They also said you had readily paid for it. Was that you?"

"No. I always settle all of my accounts at the end of the month."

"So, you handed over no cash at all?"

"None. As I said, I settle all…"

"Sir, I thank you. Might we help you back to your carriage?"

"Thank you, but no. I think I'd like to sit here a bit longer."

Back out in the fresh air, Davies took a deep breath, lifted his face to the sky, closed his eyes, stretched out his arms, then exhaled loudly as if expelling a demon.

"You alright, sir? What's next."

Davies turned to flash a reassuring smile.

"Coffee!"

*

At the counter of a small luncheonette, Davies began bombarding Donahue with theories and ideas as a means of clarifying them for himself.

Donahue was thrilled to be regarded as a colleague, not just an underling.

"I don't think we have much but, what we do have -- and have long known -- is that there's no Jack the Ripper here.

"No, sir."

"I'm also inclined to strike Alexander Miller from suspicion. Even though there is some connection, I think he was just a lost young man, crushed by powers beyond him." Davies said, a look of melancholy clouding over for a moment, then added quickly. "So, what *do* we have?"

"I'm not sure." Donahue said, struggling to answer his mentor. "Not much at all?"

Davies had to smile at Donahue's direct conclusion.

"Well yes and no."

"How so, sir?"

"We have the young woman's murder that started it all, along with a clearly connected suicide, but how we're not sure. We also have a brass button, a voice in the alley, a second murder, an attempted murder, an off-chance association, and a case of unrequited love."

"I'm not sure I know or follow all that, sir."

"Let's walk. I think better when I walk," said Davies, quickly picking up his train of thought as they exited into the street.

"We now know the identity of our victim, not a prostitute, but a society debutant on her way to Europe.

"According to Katherine Ashfield, her brother escorted Eugenia to the train station and, while we know she never got there, it also means that Ashfield and the driver that took them -- well, to wherever -- are very possibly the last people to see her alive. What you don't know, Jimmy, is that the cabbie - James LeRoy, it was - is now dead, too."

"Dead?"

"Very. About an hour ago, just outside the cab company. He recognized me, tried legging it out and was run over by a delivery wagon. Died at the scene. And I got nothing out of him. I fear we're running out of witnesses, and time."

"Why did he run?"

"Because he realized I recognized him. It was his eyes. Very unusual. Different colors - one brown, one blue. I'd seen them twice before. He was the one who shot Sean and the guy who tried to run me down last night."

"What?" Donahue exclaimed, surprised by the connection.

"Yes. So, the next question is, was LeRoy acting alone or with someone else? Our mysterious third man in the alley, perhaps?"

Davies broke off elaborating for a moment, his speech rhetorical, absorbed in an idea.

Donahue's mind was racing, trying to catch up. Davies had thrown him a lot of information he'd never heard. It was best to watch and listen.

Davies was rehearsing something even he wasn't yet sure of. Then, he began to draw out his thoughts.

"Yes, LeRoy's actions wound up being those of a man covering his crimes – and not just his crimes. He certainly hadn't planned this; certainly, wasn't acting alone. He was simply the one hired to take the Sparks girl to the train that day. His hiring might well have been quite by chance, in which case would go on to prove how every man has his price. Or it could have been that whoever hired him had the wherewithal to dig into his background or any number of potential cabbies, looking for something to exploit. In either case, the cab dispatcher said he'd come back late, gave some tale that the carriage had broken down and had to be fixed and cleaned. The company didn't even blink since LeRoy had a sum of money to pay for the time the cab was out and its repairs.

"Sparks never paid out any such sum, as you just heard. So where would a cabbie get that kind of money?"

"A robbery gone bad?" suggested Donahue, now relishing his participation…

"I don't think so. Too risky, in broad daylight, even for our Mr. LeRoy."

"A crime of passion then?"

'It very well could be.  Katherine Ashfield told me her brother and the Sparks girl had been flirtatious with one another for years. She wasn't serious; he was. On the day she was to leave, Ashfield was on the verge of proposing, but she rejected him before he had the chance. He was angry and humiliated but, somehow, still insisted he should accompany her, part way, to the rail station and drop him off at his club."

"He'll easily deny the affair meant anything to him. We have no real evidence."

"We have Miss Ashfield's words."

"Push comes to shove she'll protect her brother."

"Perhaps not. There's certainly no love-loss between the two. And given that we continue to lose witnesses, I'm wondering if even Katherine Ashfield's life could now be in danger."

Donahue abruptly stopped walking, the realization of such a danger taking him by surprise. Davies understood the reaction but continued. "We have a button."

"What about it?" Said Donahue, catching up to Davies. "Didn't McCloud say he, and even the mayor, have the same style of button, that there's a whole society that do?"

"Unfortunately, true. If it is Ashfield's -- the few run-ins I've had with his butler, convinces me, whatever garment that button was from has either been destroyed or replaced. What I do know, if it's his, it places him in that alley."

"The third man you've been referring to?"

"Exactly, but we need stronger evidence, something that puts Ashfield, definitively, in that alley on that night."

"Forgive me, but the other two men? I take it you've determined these were the cabbie LeRoy and Sean?"

"Correct."

"And how are Ashfield and Sean connected?"

"A few days after taking that fateful ride with the Sparks girl - Ashfield struck up a friendly acquaintance with Sean at Mama's place. I'm sure you know where that is. Sean worked there; Ashfield was a...well, patron.

It was now Davies who stopped walking. Donahue looked at him quizzically, coming level to him.

"Listen, there's something else to keep in mind. The day after the body turned up in the alley, there were only two people in McCloud's office, when I said I was looking for Little Sean... that I had an eyewitness who'd seen him coming out of the alley that night. Within hours of that, Sean was murdered. The two people in that room -- McCloud and Ashfield."

"Still..." began Donahue, shaking his head, then checking himself from saying the obvious. That they had no real motive, no murder weapon and that their two most significant material witnesses were dead.

Sensing Donahue's doubt and frustration Davies turned to look the constable in the eye. "I know," he said quietly. "I know."

Davies was at a loss as well. He scanned the street, looking at nothing in particular but searching for some kind of inspiration. After a moment, he seemed to find it. "I've been so stupid!"

"What do you mean?" said Donahue, startled by the inspector's sudden revelation.

Davies was on the move again but now towards their bicycles.

"Did you know that one of the businesses the Ashfields made their fortune from was the slaughter of pigs?" he said with some mounting excitement. "A while back now, but I believe the Ashfield's still own a decommissioned abattoir that's down by the old fort. Before they moved the whole operation to the junction."

"I never knew."

"Before your time, son. But I'm thinking a long-abandoned building would be the perfect place to keep a kidnap victim -- and to commit murder."

"Further, the abattoir, Ashfields' club and Union Station are in the same general area, right down toward the Lake. Ask anyone who might have witnessed LeRoy's carriage on the move the day Ashfield accompanied Miss Sparks and they'd say it was headed in the direction of his club, then the train station."

CHAPTER 30.

The shadows were getting long when Davies and Donahue rolled up to the derelict, red brick building, that sat alone on a corner lot overlooking the railway tracks.

They dismounted, leaning the bikes against a wall of the abattoir. "Ashfield & Son Meat Packers" read the weathered and rusting sign. Donahue wondered if the son was Franklin Ashfield.

Davies, quickly on the move, took several futile tugs at the chain-locked front doors, then darted off to scout the building's perimeter for any kind of alternative way in. Soon he came back around to Donahue who'd been busying himself looking for carriage tracks.

"Looks like we'll have to break in through one of these windows." Davies said, taking off his bowler.

"No tracks of any kind," offered Donahue. "It's been hot and dry for too long. The ground is like rock."

Davies took a quick look around, but the dead-end street was lifeless.

"Well, if a person was hoping to do something un-noticed, this would definitely be the place I'd choose."

He placed the top of his hat against one of the small square panes in a much larger window and, with a quick punch into it, knocked out the glass with little effort and sound. He felt for the latch and, in a quick minute, the two were standing in the dusty gloom of the vast, empty building, illuminated only by what fading daylight could make it through the banks of grimy windows.

The heat of the day and lack of any fresh air made it difficult to breathe. The temperature, Davies guessed, must've been over a hundred.

Other than their footsteps, there was no sound of any kind as they moved slowly over a floor covered with scattered straw and clumps of dirt. The space still held the faintest smell of hogs.

Donahue struck a match, which was of some small help and Davies began making his way towards what he'd barely made out to be a door.

"This looks like the main intake for the livestock," Davies surmised. "Over here must've been where they'd slaughter."

"Not much left behind," noted Donahue, striking another match as Davies pulled opened the door to a room that wasn't quite so dim owing to a large west facing window.

Davies could make out that the entire floor, as well as the bottom half of the walls, were tiled in white ceramic.

*Yes, easy to clean blood from.*

He went down on one knee and ran a hand across the floor, finding it virtually dirt and dust-free. Davies dropped his head feeling defeated. Even at first glance, he knew deep down, they wouldn't find anything.

"Donahue," he called back.

"You find something sir?" Donahue said, rushing into the room.

"A very clean floor. Too clean, in fact, for a room that supposedly hadn't been used in years. I wouldn't doubt this whole room has been scrubbed quite recently. We won't find anything here." He stood and exhaled loudly in frustration.

"It's like we were just a few steps behind, sir."

"And why not? Our man has had the benefit of three whole days to get ahead of us. Let's get the hell out of here. I can't breathe for the heat."

Back on the street, the light of day was almost gone. Davies' mood had turned grim, and Donahue could only wait in silence as the inspector paced about, looking worried and distant.

"Well, this was a bust." Davies finally said. "We've still got to place Ashfield in that alleyway. I've also still got another longshot and may be able to use it to push him, but we're going to have to get Ashfield back to division and into an interrogation room."

"You can't mean now, sir. It's getting late."

Davies looked to the sky, then down the darkening streets. Yes. This day was gone.

Suddenly, he felt heavy and a parched nagging form at the back of his throat. Unconsciously, he reached for his tin. Fear of the long, empty hours to come gave him the shivers.

He pulled out his notebook and pencil and quickly wrote a few words, ripped out the page, folded it, then handed it to Donahue.

"Drop by division on your way home and book the interrogation room, in my name, for 10 a.m. First thing in the morning, take this to Ashfield, telling him I request his presence at division, that I have a few questions for him. Get back to division and, if I'm not there yet, wait for Ashfield's arrival and get him to the interrogation room. Use the alley entrance at the back, we don't want any prying eyes. Thankfully, McCloud has his morning meeting with the Mayor and the Chief, so we should have a few uninterrupted hours. And hopefully I'll have someone with me who can place Ashfield in that alley."

"Where are you going now, sir?"

"Gotta visit my old pal Joe Levy. I'm hoping he can give me a little info about the Ashfield family business. Then, I can't say." Davies said, making a move to his bike. "And don't look so worried, son," he added, throwing a leg over the saddle, and pushing off, heading out into the evening.

Donahue waited until the inspector was out of sight before unfolding and reading the note. Smiling, he tucked it into his breast pocket.

Davies had cycled away from Donahue at a pace, knowing Mama's medicine wasn't going to help this time. The beast was back and angry, feeding on his self-doubt.

He knew he was going to lie to himself, knew he was going to tell himself he could have just one. To steady himself, to get through this.

He was up against it now, though. He knew how this night was going to end, even as he sped along, trying to convince himself it wouldn't.

CHAPTER 31.

Donahue was rocking on his heels in the great foyer of the Ashfield house, scanning the high ceiling and wondering just how much the Ashfields had to be worth when Franklin Ashfield, obviously terribly per-turbed, blustered his way down the staircase.

"Constable, what can it possibly be now? This is annoying at the best of times but now is far, far too early for this nonsense."

"Apologies, sir, but Inspector Davies has charged me with… well, requesting, your presence at division. He has some questions he'd like answered."

"Really, this is too much." Ashfield said, almost laughing, trying his best to feint disbelief. "He was here less than 24 hours ago, when he showed scant regard for me, absolutely no respect. In my own home! Where were these questions yesterday?"

Donahue stood stone-faced, saying nothing.

"Well, you can tell your inspector…"

"He asked me to give you this," said Donahue, presenting the note from his pocket.

Ashfield unfolded and read it. To Donahue's eye, all the color drained from his face for a moment and was stumped as to how to respond. Ashfield suddenly decided displaying some alarm and bluster would seem appropriate.

"What does he mean by this? Is she alright?"

Donahue shook his head, looked innocently at Ashfield, and shrugged. "I haven't read the note, sir, and I don't know who you're referring to. All I know is that I'm here to get you to come to division."

"Well, good thing my carriage is all ready to go, the horses harnessed."

*

Ifan turned off Louisa and walked into the alley-way where he was first introduced to Eugenia Sparks, feeling just as hungover and shattered as he was that day.

It had been a long time since he and Joe Levy had pulled an all-nighter, it felt good to work like that again. But a nagging doubt turned, as it does, into a drinking bout. Now he was just hoping it would all be enough.

The graffiti had been scrubbed from the wall and refuse cluttered the area where her body had been left. As if she had never been here. No mob of press, no police, no gawkers. Just garbage.

Passing the spot where he'd found the button, he rapped on the gate to the yard where he'd spoken with the Chinese woman four days earlier. The bed was still there; the woman wasn't.

"Hello, is anybody there? Hello!"

Getting no response, Davies stretched his arm over the gate and sprung the latch. As the gate scraped open, he was suddenly confronted by the blank stare of a dirty-faced barefoot child.

"Oh, hello again. It's Li Jing, isn't it? You remember me? I was here asking you and your mum some questions a while back…about the men in the alley. You remember?"

The child nodded, not really caring one way or another why the silly man was back.

"Is your mum home?"

The girl simply shook her head, her silence beginning to unsettle Davies whose hangover had started to pound behind his eyes.

Expecting the worst, he could only ask: "Right. Li Jing, do you know when she'll be back?"

"She ain't comin' back. She died," the girl finally spoke, the memory of the event flickering behind her eyes as she hardened herself against the telling. "And people call me Susie."

"Li Jing, ah, Susie, I'm sorry."

"It's okay. She doesn't hurt anymore."

"Yes," Davies nodded, otherwise at a loss for words before the child, who no longer looked like a child. That part of her was leaving the day they'd met.

Life for the children of the Ward aged them, robbed them. By ten they were small adults. This was common ground for both he and the girl. If you didn't die of disease, hunger, and neglect, even violence, you came of age fast, hardened against the world and those in it.

With neither knowing what else to say, they shrugged their not knowing at one another and Susie turned to go back in.

"Susie," Davies suddenly recalled why he'd come. "Do you think you could recognize the voice you heard in the alleyway that night? If you heard it again?"

"Dunno."

"Would you be able to come to where I work and try?"

"Okay."

"Is your father here or someone else to let them know where you'll be?" "Nope," she said, offering up her hand for Davies to take.

"Did you eat today?"

She shook her head.

"Well, we'll fix that," he said, and the unlikely pair headed out of the yard, scraping the gate closed behind them.

CHAPTER 32.

Ashfield had a few choice words for Donahue - really directed at the thought of Davies - before dismissing him and storming from the foyer, yelling for his butler.

Donahue had ridden as hard as he could to gain whatever time he might need back at division. Given how pissed Ashfield had been, it could be as few as 10 minutes, 15 tops.

He first checked in with the morning desk sergeant, advising him that Davies was enroute and would need the interview room shortly.

"Confidential stuff, so, we'll be using the back entrance," he explained. "I'll take care of it."

He then headed for a much-needed smoke, pacing the sidewalk, more

than a little anxious for which of Ashfield or Davies would show first.

He was hoping for Davies but no such luck, as a carriage reeled round a corner and headed his way. His heart beat a little faster and the nerves kicked in. "Where the hell is Davies!" Ashfield demanded, stepping out almost before the horses had come to a full stop.

Donahue dropped his cigarette, crushing it with his boot, and was about to answer when Davies came up behind him, Susie in tow.

"Ah, excellent, Donahue, you were able to entice Mr. Ashfield to come in."

"What the hell is the meaning of this note, Davies?" Ashfield said, brandishing it.

"Language, we have a young person here."

"Who's this?" Ashfield spat out, waving a dismissive hand, not really seeing the girl in his temper.

"This is Susie. Say hello, Susie."

Susie offered a shy "hello" then slid behind Davies' leg, keeping watchful and wide eyes on Ashfield.

"No need to hide. This is the Right Honorable Mr. Ashfield. He works for the people. I'm sure he'd like to say hello to you."

Ashfield tipped his hat and grudgingly managed some limp acknowledgement.

"Shall we?" Davies said, gesturing toward the alley that led behind the

division. Seeing Ashfield's hesitation, Davies reassured him that the back entrance was in his own best interest, no prying eyes and all.

*

The group stepped into a dimly-lit hallway that led to a closed door at one end and, at a farther distance in the other direction, the sergeant's desk, and the mounting morning hubbub.

Davies handed Susie off to Donahue telling him, "find a place for her to wait. I'll be out shortly," he said, adding, "oh, try and find some shoes for her in the lost and found."

Entering the interview room, Davies lit a single gas lamp illuminating an unflattering room of drab beige, with no windows. Nothing hung on the walls and just a few wooden chairs were tucked into a plain, worn desk.

"Again, I ask you, what the is the meaning of this?" Ashfield dramatically tossed the note to the table, revealing what Davies had written: Eugenia Sparks.

Calmly but pointedly, Davies offered Ashfield a seat. For his part, Ashfield seemed agitated, looking about nervously, unsure what the game was.

Davies smiled and with a cursory, mercurial look to the door, leaned in, lowered his voice, and set about giving the appearance of taking Ashfield into his confidence.

"Look, I didn't tell your sister this, but we've determined the identity of our Jane Doe from the Ward. I believe you and your sister knew the young lady, Eugenia Sparks?"

Davies tapped the note for effect.

For a moment, Ashfield didn't react; in the next, a pained expression overtook him. Removing his hat and placing it on the table he reached for his handkerchief and dabbed his brow.

"Didn't think you ever sweat," observed Davies.

"Exceptional times inspector."

In the silence that followed, the two nodded at one another, waiting.

Patiently, Davies watched as Ashfield gathered himself, then…

"Oh God, that's horrible. I'm glad you didn't tell Katherine, they were such good friends, she'll be devastated."

"You knew Miss Sparks quite well too, didn't you?"

"Of course."

"How well?"

Ashfield eyed Davies with a certain wariness yet didn't answer right away. He was mulling something and, having cooled his lingering agitation, had weighed what to say.

"If you must know, I wanted to marry Eugenia. I know my sister informed you of this fact. Also, that she refused me."

"That must have upset you, made you angry?"

"Are you accusing me of something? Do I need to call for my lawyer?"

"Lawyer?" Davies suppressed a smile, spreading his arms wide. "That's rather defensive. I'm just asking a few questions here."

Ashfield leaned back in his chair staring at Davies, then letting out an exasperated breath, said "fine."

"When was the last time you saw Miss Sparks?", Davies resumed, reading his notebook.

"I left her, quite alive, in a cab we shared. I had asked her to drop me off at my club on her way to the train station the day she was to leave for Europe. Again, as you no doubt already know."

"Yes, I also know you left your club sometime mid-afternoon, then what?"

"I walked home."

"Walked home? Why didn't you take your carriage?"

"I was a little... I just felt like a walk."

"Did anyone see you?"

"I assume many people saw me in a big city. Look, I left Eugenia with the cabbie who was to help her at the train station."

"And he would be able to corroborate this?" Davies pressed. "Do you happen to know the name of this cabbie?"

"Why would I know the name of…" Ashfield stopped abruptly. He paused, and again weighed his thoughts.

Davies looked up from his notes, waiting for Ashfield to continue.

Davies had worried over – but didn't let show - that Katherine had spoken of their conversation. He figured that would happen but to what extent had she been coerced? Had he put her in harm's way? He feared for her safety, what retribution she might face.

"His name is LeRoy, the cabbie." Ashfield finally blurted out in a clipped manner, "I believe the company is Hazelton. I'm sure he could confirm I left him to help with Eugenia after dropping me off." He dabbed his brow again.

"Do you remember what time you got back home, who was there?"

"I don't remember the time, but it was late. My butler and sister were at home, but she'd already retired for the evening."

"It took you some time to get home."

"It's a long walk and I'm not as young or as quick as I once was."

"Can the butler or your sister confirm the time you came in?"

"I'm sure my butler can but my sister, as you know, takes laudanum for her nerves. I doubt she heard anything. Look, I've answered your questions. If there's anything else, I feel my lawyer should be involved, yes?"

Davies looked up from his notebook, this time as if he had forgotten something, then abruptly got to his feet, swiftly moving to the door.

"Sorry, I need to have a quick word with someone. I'll be right back."

Ashfield sat stunned. Before he had time to protest, he heard Davies had locked the door behind him.

In the hallway, Davies needed to lean for a moment, his hangover raging, trying to keep his head together. He'd have to explain, or lie, why he just locked the door.

*Cross that bridge later.*

Donahue was sitting with Susie across from the sergeant's desk, trying an ill-fitting pair of shoes on the girl, who looked unimpressed, if not pained. Pulling himself together, Davies strode over.

The desk sergeant, busy with some paperwork, glanced up briefly with a quizzical look, catching Davies as he sidled up to Donahue speaking in a low tone.

"I need you to follow me into the room after I have a quick chat with Susie here." Davies flashed Susie a smile. "Ashfield's starting to think he needs a lawyer. I need to keep him in that room, talking, if I can. Maybe with you at the door he'll feel a little more intimidated. It's worth a shot, it's now or never. I've got to push him."

Donahue nodded and, giving up on the shoes, made his way down the hall.

Davies turned to Susie, nervous to ask his questions. It was obvious he was desperate.

"Susie, were you able to recognize the voice from the alley? Think back, was that the man? Was it his voice?" Davies said, pointing toward the interrogation room.

*

Ashfield was standing, stretching his legs when Davies got back to the room, Donahue at his heels. Ashfield's anger flashed and, snatching his hat from the table, stepped into Davies.

"Why the devil did you lock the door?" he huffed, now making to exit. "I'll be reporting this to McCloud. I don't think you realize who you're speaking to!"

"A servant of the people, that's who" Davies said, coolly, "and I'm sure you'll be quick to report to McCloud. The thing is, I have a conundrum."

"What's that? Why should I care about your conundrum?"

"I'm not exactly sure, Mr. Ashfield. You know the young girl that I came in with?"

"I don't *know* her, but yes."

"She's just said the most incredible thing. Maybe you can help me out here."

"What?" Ashfield said, impatient for Davie's to get to his point and leave off fishing. Shaking his head, he moved to leave but, seeing Donahue standing astride the door, grew confused and stopped.

"She claims" said Davies, "she recognized your voice from the night Eugenia Sparks' body was dumped in the alley."

Ashfield's face lost all color briefly but shaking this off, adjusted his demeanor to that of amused disbelief.

"You see," Davies continued, "she was tending to her sick mother in back of their shack that sits almost in the alley itself, when she says she heard your voice, with two others."

"That's absurd."

"Yes, yes, I'm sure she must be mistaken, but if you don't mind, could you tell me where you were that night?"

"What night."

Davies flipped back some pages of his notebook and scanned, letting the moment drag out as Ashfield shifted his weight from left to right.

"That would be the night of… Tuesday, July 9th.

"I believe I was at home. Again, my butler can verify that." Ashfield began to pace, tightening the grip on his hat with both hands, trying to contain his anger.

"Anyone else?"

"No. I let all other staff go after dinner."

"I must ask again, your sister?"

"She was asleep." Ashfield retorted.

"What time did she go to bed? She may've gotten up in the night and heard you. It wouldn't hurt to ask her?"

"How many times do I have to repeat, she was asleep." Ashfield about hissed at Davies, clenching his jaw.

"Right, right." Davies now changed his tone, and the subject.

"Incredible this heat, huh? Hottest on record apparently. Did you know 28 people died in one day due to the heat?"

"I'm sure that is infinitely fascinating inspector, the weather, but I'm a busy man."

"Yes, of course. I wonder, Mr. Ashfield, how long do you think a person would last, say, in a stifling hot room, temperatures over a hundred degrees?"

"I wouldn't know." Ashfield slowly sat down again, reconciled to wait out Davies' musings. Taking a quick glance to Donahue, standing unmoved at the door, he added carefully, "and why do you ask?"

"Well, we believe Miss Sparks was detained, no, held captive in such a room. Her killer couldn't have known it would get so deadly hot. She was likely dead by the time…you get the idea."

Ashfield had grown silent. Davies, looking to capitalize, moved a chair close to him and, talking freely, honestly, man to man, began to feed the story of Eugenia Sparks' last moments, as he had interpreted the evidence to that point.

"You see, I think her killer was surprised to find her in a dehydrated state, probably delirious, close to death, if not dead already. He couldn't call a doctor or go to the nearest hospital. He didn't mean to kill her; it was an accident."

Ashfield had closed his eyes, his head slightly nodding listening to Davies, the color draining from him as if he might be sick.

"Are you alright, Mr. Ashfield?"

Without opening his eyes, Ashfield replied with a simple, "mm hmm."

Again, Davies switched up, sat back in his chair with ease but with eyes locked on Ashfield.

"Funny, it's a mystery to me and perhaps you can help me out with this other conundrum. After I revealed to both you and McCloud that 'little' Sean was a person of interest, suddenly he's gunned down in the street."

"What's are you trying to say, inspector?" Ashfield seemed to come to, his eyes opening quizzically at Davies's implication.

"Well, you were the only two who knew that specific information."

"Coincidence, I'm sure."

"I suppose it's also coincidence that the man who shot Sean also tried to run me over."

"How would you know that?" Ashfield said, perking up a bit in his seat.

"I was within 10 feet of him both times. He's got a very distinctive pair of eyes, one blue, one brown. I wouldn't miss those if I saw them again."

"This is all very interesting, inspector, but what has it got to do with me?"

Ashfield had now gathered himself. Whatever briefly ailed him had now passed. He sat up. Davies' focus sharpened in expectation.

"Like I said, you were one of two people who knew that information."

"And like I said, coincidence."

Davies smiled and was about to continue when, from the other side of the door, raised voices were heard coming from the sergeant's desk.

"McCloud!" Donahue interrupted.

"Bloody hell," Davies mumbled, hearing McCloud's yell precede him down the hall.

"Davies!"

*

"What's going on here?," McCloud stormed in, his face taking on the usual redness.

"Thank you for getting here so quickly, William," said Ashfield with a note of bitter sarcasm. "How's the Mayor?"

Davies realized that, of course, Ashfield would have contacted McCloud before leaving home and thinking quickly, figured it better to go on the offensive, rather than wait for McCloud to blow his top.

"Sir, if you don't mind, I'm conducting an inter-view."

"An interview?"

"Mr. Ashfield here is acquainted with, or was acquainted with, our Jane Doe from the Ward. A Miss Eugenia Sparks and a friend of the Ashfield family. I'm merely trying to ascertain Mr. Ashfield's whereabouts on the night…"

"Which I've already explained to you." Ashfield interrupted, getting to his feet, relieved an ally was now in the room.

"Please, sit down, Mr. Ashfield. I've not finished." Davies demanded.

"Are you charging me with something?"

"No, but I am prepared to make this a formal interview request."

"Then I shall require my lawyer. William, is this how your department treats members of parliament? Trickery and obfuscation."

"I remind you, sir, you came here of your own free will." Davies said, adding, "And I never obfuscated in my life!"

"Gentlemen!" McCloud had had enough, glaring at Davies with resentment for putting him in this situation. "Apologies, Franklin. Now, inspector Davies, again what the hell is going on."

"Sir, I'm just trying to clarify the whereabouts of Mr. Ashfield on the night Miss Sparks' body was dumped in the alley. I've uncovered a witness that could *put* Mr. Ashfield in the alley at that time."

Davies knew he was stretching the idea of a witness. He was counting on

McCloud's investigative curiosity to be pricked, allowing him to press forward.

"Witness!," boomed Ashfield. "Some little Chink kid who *thinks* she heard my voice. My attorney will make short work of that."

"I don't think it'll get that far, Franklin." McCloud placated. "Davies, are you suggesting Mr. Ashfield had something to do with this murder?"

"Sir, there is enough doubt and suspicion to warrant further investigation," Davies pressed harder now. "Mr. Ashfield hasn't given me a satisfactory answer and I now wish to, again, interview his sister to ascertain what time, if at all, he returned home that night. Mr. Ashfield, however, is resistant." Davies took a breath, looking at McCloud who was thinking this out, stunned at the news he'd just heard. McCloud then glanced at Ashfield who was glaring.

"Well, Franklin, if it clears this up...?"

"I wish I could, William, but Katherine is already on her way to Europe, she left yesterday." Ashfield pulled his watch from his pocket. "She'll be sailing by now."

Davies stepped back, stung, "what?" The room lost air. The fear Davies had for Miss Ashfield's safety was now becoming manifest, though, still unclear.

"And why's that, Franklin?" McCloud leaned in, his curiosity and frustration starting to bubble.

"Yes, Mr. Ashfield. Why have you packed your sister off?"

"I haven't 'packed her off,'" said Ashfield, pulling a piece of paper from his jacket pocket and unfolding it for McCloud to read.

"This is a doctor's certificate to have Katherine committed for hysteria. I was advised by our doctor that this hospital in Belgium was the best facility in the world. No matter what you think of me, inspector Davies, I will do everything in my power to help my sister recover."

Again, Davies was put back on his heels; again, Ashfield a step ahead of him. His mind whirred. He couldn't let Ashfield leave this room without getting the truth out of him. All he'd managed at first was a weak, "that's convenient."

Calming his racing mind with a breath, Davies looked in Ashfeild's eyes with cold certainty and played his last card.

"A friend in the press dug up something interesting. Told me you're deep in debt Mr. Ashfield, in fact, you're pretty much bankrupt. I think you desperately needed Eugenia Sparks to marry you, well, you needed her family's money. How you would get a hold of it, somehow, became complicated by her unfortunate death."

"What's that?" McCloud said, turning to Ashfield, who stood silent and blinking. No one moved.

Then snorting with contempt Ashfield said, "the press…"

A knock at the door broke the spell in the tense room, followed by the desk sergeant entering, holding a report.

"Sorry to interrupt, sir. We've got an ID on that cabbie who was run over."

"Not now, sergeant!" McCloud waved him off, with a preoccupied ferocity.

The sergeant bit his tongue. Better than blurting out what was truly on his mind, he decided to offer a polite reminder that the inspector had specifically asked to be informed right away, since the accident had involved inspector Davies.

*This was too much! No, he can't be this lucky!* Davies' mind whirled.

His heart pounding, Davies jumped in to usher the sergeant out, trying to cut him off before he uttered the name.

Donahue, who had been dumb-struck through most of the encounter, twigged at the same moment and moved quickly to aid Davies. The sergeant, just doing his duty, stood bewildered, not moving.

Ashfield smiled and, sensing an opportunity, raised his voice over the fracas, stopping everyone.

"Who was this cabbie? His name?"

The sergeant looked to McCloud and, getting a nod, opened the file to read: "James LeRoy is the name of the deceased, sir."

"Thank you, sergeant." And with that McCloud dismissed him.

"James LeRoy! That's the cabbie I told inspector Davies of, the one I left to help Eugenia." Ashfield said, a light in his eyes twinkling, smelling blood in the water. "He's the last to see her alive. He's your man!"

From that moment, Davies felt stuck in quicksand, events unfolding in slow motion, as if in a foggy dream.

He could see it all being laid out in front of him – and, no doubt, in McCloud's mind as well. Ashfield was defining the narrative, planting seeds.

LeRoy had been an opportunist, seizing the girl, perhaps for ransom, a kidnapping gone wrong. It went too far, and she ended up dead. Not knowing what to do, LeRoy panicked, eventually lighting on the idea of the Ripper.

In the next moment, the room exploded. Striking out, trying to grasp any kind of control, Davies pushed Ashfield back into his chair. He could hear his own voice but was unable to stem the flow of abuse, as if he had become disembodied and was watching from above.

If he had been clear, not suffering a hangover in this stifling room, he could have rebutted, turned McCloud to the truth. Instead, rage and frustration had taken hold, and he was now on the man almost physically trying to drag a confession out of him.

Ashfield fired back. "How dare you lay hands on a member of parliament!"

"You're an MP for Christ's sake, not a fucking king." Davies growled.

"McCloud, get your man off me! I'll be making a formal complaint and expect charges to be laid. This inspector better be relieved of his duties," Ashfield said, struggling against Davies' hold.

Standing over Ashfield, gripping the lapels of his jacket, Davies knew he had gone too far. The die was cast. He felt sick as Donahue pulled him off.

"You two, get out!" Yelled McCloud, pointing to both Davies and Donahue. "Davies, you're suspended as of now!"

"For what?"

"Striking a member of parliament. You'll be lucky if you're not charged."

A faint, almost imperceptible smile twitched at the corners of McCloud's lips. He wouldn't have to worry about Davies anymore.

*He's done it to himself.*

Donahue had Davies by both elbows, dragging him towards the door while Davies, feeling there was nothing left to lose, let loose a final barrage of profanity.

McCloud followed tight to the two, giving Davies a dismissive push to his chest to get him into the hall then slammed the door. Davies caught one final glimpse of Ahsfield, a malicious, victorious grin spreading across his self-satisfied face.

In the hallway, Davies pushed Donahue off and, with a "get off," stormed down the hall and out of the building, leaving a stunned Donahue looking after him.

Catching the eye of the forgotten Susie, still patiently waiting, Donahue felt a heaviness overcome him.

He walked over to her. "You hungry?"

*

Stumbling out into the heat, Davies about screamed. Clenching his fist, and bringing it to his mouth, he bit into his forefinger, which stopped him from emptying out his guts right there.

Putting some distance between him and division, he tucked into an opening between buildings, wretched, wiped his mouth, then lit a cigarette. The nausea slowly eased off.

*Lord help me*, he thought. *They've kicked me off the case and there'll be a disciplinary hearing and a suspension, if not charges.* Whatever Ashfield's telling McCloud, it didn't look good for him - or the case.

*Never go up against an MP, and a rich one at that.*

Taking a few more hauls then flicking his butt to the gutter he headed toward the heart of the Ward.

Once again, he found himself standing across the street from the Chinese laundry. He stood there contemplating. Now and then he paced, looked up to the window, trying to figure if he was going to go in or not.

CHAPTER 33.

Donahue was half-numb, in shock, as he led Susie home in the early-afternoon heat. *What had just happened? How does Ashfield simply walk free?* He assumed this would be the outcome after watching Ashfield and McCloud walk out of the interview room like two old chums from prep school. McCloud's deference was nauseating, an image Donahue wouldn't forget.

The unlikely pair strolled hand in hand, Donahue at least thankful she was the silent type. The kid absent-mindedly nibbled at the last corner of a sandwich Donahue had managed to dig up for her. She looked about, here and there, without emotion or care, not once up at Donahue. To her, he was nothing more than another grown-up passing through her hard, sad young life.

*He's guilty. I know he is.*

Donahue wasn't sure if he'd said that out loud or not. Nor would it matter since they'd arrived at the front of the alley off Louisa. She pulled her hand out of his and ran off. He blurted, "Bye, Susie," but she never turned back and soon disappeared.

*

Donahue was similarly confused as to why he'd even decided to return to division.

Entering the squad room, he was taken off guard by the broad smiles of many of his fellow constables.

Some offered a pat on the back with their congratulations. There might have been a touch of envy in some, but most seemed genuinely curious for details.

He found out, was told, that he was considered a hero for helping, first, to identify Eugenia Sparks as the young murder victim, then, soon after, Jack the Ripper copycat killer, cabbie James LeRoy.

Donahue was stunned. What had taken place since he'd left with Susie? Jack the Ripper copycat? The dime dropped. So, that's how they're going to play this. He could only nod. Couldn't speak, couldn't force a smile of acknowledgement.

He walked to his desk. There, sitting on top waiting for him was a report folder. Slowly he opened the file.

In McCloud's bold hand it was laid out for him - the investigation and evidence for the case that James LeRoy was the murderer of Eugenia Sparks, the Ripper copycat.

As Donahue stood there absorbed, reading in disbelief. He suddenly had the feeling he was being observed. Looking up, he scanned the room settling on the glass windows of McCloud's office. The man was standing there. They locked eyes and his stomach turned as McCloud nodded slowly at him, the intent clear. He was being obliged to sign.

Sign the statement and he'd be a hero, maybe even get a promotion. If not, too bad, it was going to be reported this way and there was nothing he could do about it.

Donahue found a pen, dipped it and, with all his mounting self-hatred, held it over the document. As the pen wavered there, he had a flash of those foolish, naive dreams of becoming a great and honorable detective and was overwhelmed with shame. Singing, he would be forever tarnished. He'd enter the world of the broken and cynical, that place inhabited by the likes of McCloud and Davies and so many others beside.

Looking around, the room was now back to normal on a day that would continue as all the other days had before it. Would this news help the Sparks family with their loss and pain? Would just having a name be enough? Could they care who really murdered their child? Would anybody care who Franklin Ashfield really was?

Donahue's own thoughts and justifications revolted him. The world would continue without a clue of the truth, a self-satisfied McCloud watching from behind his glass walls.

He lowered the pen, placing it in its resting spot, took up the file and tossed it into the waste bin under his desk. He again caught McCloud's eye but, this time, McCloud let loose the blinds, blocking him out.

In what felt like an eternity, Donahue turned and took the short walk to the sign-in board. He looked up to where his name was printed in chalk and, with a lump in his throat, moved the peg from "signed in" to "signed out."

CHAPTER 34.

Ifan shivered as he felt cool steel placed next to his temple and heard the hammer of a pistol being cocked.

*Fair enough*, he thought. He had just barged through Mama's door unannounced. He glanced over his shoulder and took in the calm, yet psychopathic, face of the young bouncer, now waiting on her order to shoot him or not.

Mama waved off her boy, coolly studied Ifan from her chair, cracking and popping peanuts into her mouth a few at a time.

"You look like shit. Are you're high?"

Ifan nodded, then shuffled his body over to his usual seat, plopping down heavy, sweating, and reeking of stale booze and hash.

Mama waited as he shifted and fidgeted uncomfortably.

"What's on your mind?"

"I just got myself suspended and possibly worse."

"Want a drink?"

"No."

"So, what happened?"

"They got me." he said, searching for his tobacco tin, then leaving off in frustration. "That old boys' club got me."

"Welcome to the world."

"I thought I was ahead of him but, in reality, he played me like a fish on a line."

"Who?"

"Ashfield," Davies paused, then, in a flood, let go. "I found out yesterday. I was checking out his family's old, closed-up, abattoir. My gut was screaming. I knew it was where he'd kept the girl but then, when I saw it, all scrubbed so clean, not a sign of anything. I'd never find evidence there.

We were always a few steps behind him.

Levy and I worked hard, but the doubts kept coming. I knew I was grasping...I knew something was gonna happen to Miss Ashfield if I didn't come up with something. Then, I got drunk. I couldn't...it all felt too much, like nothing would stick to this man. I threw up a prayer to the Mother Mary. Then again today, steps ahead, getting his sister out of the country. And luck! Le Roy, everything played into his hands."

Ifan was now just throwing out disconnected events and names, no longer making sense. Mama leaned in, placing a hand lightly on his knee. He twitched at the touch of it and fell silent again.

"And so, you come to see me?"

"I've been chewing on something for a while now. Maybe you can help me out."

"Depends."

"I know Ashfield's a regular customer of yours," before Mama could duck the claim, Ifan stopped her, "don't deny it. What I need to know is how often. Does he have any kinks, anything I can use against him?"

"You gotta let it go. This man's got you crazy."

Mama looked to her side table where a half-smoked cigar sat in the ashtray. She re-lit it, letting the match fall into the ashtray with a light 'clink.'

"I need your help Mamma."

"Now, why would I tell you something like that? You know my discretion is what keeps me in business. I like high-paying customers. They get what they want, and I stay off the streets, or worse."

"If there's something juicy?" Davies leaned in so close to Mama, she could feel his desperation. "Maybe I can work it that nothing blows back on you."

"And how are you going to achieve that kind of miracle?"

"What if a raid was conducted by a know-nothing rookie, acting alone, who just happens to know what room Ashfield's in. Also suppose one of my press buddies happens to be here when it all goes down and writes a scandalous front-page splash. We make sure you're nowhere in sight and the press keeps your name out of it."

"But you know *they'll* know." She said, wanting to stress the gravity, and danger of his proposal.

Frustrated, Ifan sat back in his chair scratching the few days stubble on his cheek as he thought. He knew she was protecting herself, but he couldn't let it end this way.

"You want to know what he did to that young woman, because he felt slighted, thinking he had a right to possess her and her money?"

"Men've been doing that for centuries, baby. Where do you think you are? Look where you're sitting. In a whore house."

"You want to get something back?... I can't put him away but, between us, we can hurt him in the place I know he fears most being judged, his much-valued status in society."

Mama's eyes narrowed to slits as she weighed what he was asking, but still said nothing. Seeing that Mama could go either way, Davies thought he'd give a nudge.

"We'll take care of you."

"Who's we?"

"I got a kid inside the force. I'll keep informed. We'll hide you away till it all blows over."

"I'll have to start over. It's gonna cost me."

"Ya, it will."

Mama took another long haul from her cigar as she pondered, not taking her eyes from Ifan's that looked so pleading.

"I always hated that son-of-a bitch."

Opening her side table's hidden drawer, where she'd once drawn a ball of hash, Mama pulled out a black notebook. Flipping through the first few pages, she stopped and scanned down a list of names.

"He does have a particular appetite," she said, handing the notebook to him.

"Holy shit." Ifan mumbled, looking back to Mama as if to make sure he was seeing right.

"Yes."

"Well, well. Looks like he's gonna be here on Saturday."

"That's right."

"Can you make sure you're disappeared when he visits?" Ifan stood energetically, life coming back into him. "Can I take this with me? I see a few names here that might not like me knowing what they're up to, could come in handy at my hearing."

"Don't lose it, it's my security."

"If he changes plans let me know through Mickey Doolan. I don't trust anyone at division."

"What about your rookie?"

"The less he knows the better. Nothing can slip out that way." He said, making his way to the exit.

"This could fuck me, Ifan!" Mama yelled after him, but he had already cleared the door.

*

Joe Levy was sitting at his desk in the Toronto Star building, sweating. No matter how hard he tried, he couldn't get enough windows open to create any kind of a cross-breeze. He was banging out and putting the finishing touches on the next day's sensation due by the end of the day, when he felt someone hovering over him. He looked up to see the flushed, smiling face of Ifan Davies, all but busting with excitement. Something good for him, he hoped.

"Well, you gonna stand there dripping sweat on my copy, or tell me why you're grinning like an idiot?"

"How would you like a nice, front-page exclusive, guaranteed to rip the lid off a certain politician's life."

Levy looked at his copy, shook his head with a slight self-conscious laugh, then turned back to Davies.

"What about the Ripper?"

"Oh, you're gonna hear about that soon enough but not from me."

The two stared at one another in a suspended moment of anticipation, slowly breaking into a smile. Levy suddenly jumped up, grabbed his jacket off the back of his chair, ripped the finished copy from his type-writer and pointed to the exit.

"Lead on, McDuff!"

CHAPTER 35.

Ifan quietly knocked on the door across the hall from his own little hovel. Hearing it unlocked, he pushed it open only enough to slide inside.

"I brought you something to eat." he said, placing a paper-wrapped bundle on a small table that stood beside the bed. The room was pretty much identical to his, a bit cleaner, and there were no windows facing the street. Just how he wanted it. In a place like this, a person can disappear. Nobody, not even the cops make their way here, not unless someone gets killed.

"You go to the Chinese place again?"

"Ya, they think I've got a big appetite for their food."

"Maybe something different tomorrow, okay."

"Sure."

"How is it out there, what's the word on the street?"

"So far, it's quiet. My rookie says McCloud doesn't want anything to do with it anymore and Ashfield's left the country."

"That's good news." Mama said, relaxing enough to move from the window she'd been spying out of, peeking from behind the curtains. She pulled up a chair and unwrap her food. "How're my girls?"

"Mikey's gott'em stashed in the rooms above his place. Everybody's laying low."

"He better not take advantage."

Ifan grinned and nodded, opening the door a crack.

"You need anything before I go?"

"No, thank you Ifan." Mama greedily dug into her food with not much else to say. Davies gave the hallway another quick survey then slipped out.

*

Ifan, cautiously, took the few steps down into Doolan's. From door to bar, muddy, wet footprints covered the floor, making the stone slick. It had rained the night before and into the morning, finally breaking the oppressive heat and humidity of the last few weeks.

Doolan had his back to the door when Ifan came in, turning to see him pull a newspaper from under his arm and place it for him on the bar.

Mickey unfolded it and lay it flat. Stepping square to the bar, he rested his hands on the rail, read the headline and nodded his approval.

"Your man at the paper done a good job there. I would've preferred killing the foocker, though."

"Ya, but it's a hangin' offence, Mickey."

"Only if you's catch me."

"Not me, they want to kick me off the force. We'll see what happens at the disciplinary hearing. I've got an Ace or two yet to play."

"Have you now?" Mickey lifted the paper eye level and read out loud:

"'FEDERAL MP FRANKLIN ASHFIELD, FOUND IN HOUSE OF ILL-REPUTE WITH YOUNG MALE PROSTITUTE DURING LATE-NIGHT RAID.'"

"Oh, ho, brilliant," chuckled Doolan, giving Davies a wry sideways smile. "I think this deserves a drink."

"Not your shite stout."

"Shite stout? Let me tell you, it's the best you'll find this side of the Atlantic."

Davies dug for his tobacco and Doolan stepped behind the bar when the door opened to a pair of back-lit figures.

"Look what I found hanging about out front," boomed the jovial voice of

Joe Levy, who was giving Donahue a light-hearted push toward the bar.

"A coupla stouts lads?"

Levy was immediately delighted to accept; Donahue declined, being on duty and all.

"As if that ever stopped a copper, Jimmy," Doolan cackled.

"Didn't kick you off the force then?" Ifan grunted, turning to face Donahue.

"No. Desk duty. The disciplinary hearing didn't find my actions regarding the raid to be overstepped. I think they were afraid I might've found out some of them frequent the place."

"Did ya?" Levy's journo instinct perking up.

"And, what's now called the LeRoy case? Well, McCloud just wants it to all go away." Said Donahue, sidestepping Levy's question, fearing the leverage he enjoyed could be lost by a stray comment.

"It and me." Ifan said, with a touch of bitterness that surprised him. He wondered if it had been Donahue's good luck or the very real possibility, he could lose the only job he ever wanted, that stung most. He twinged at the memory of yelling in Ashfield's face and couldn't help thinking he'd thrown it all away.

He could hear the ongoing banter deep in the background, but Ifan was far away and up in his head. Until shaking off his melancholy to get himself back in the room.

Doolan threw down four pints on the bar, Donahue again protested, was easily won over, and all four men took large gulps.

There was a moment of awkward silence, each not sure what to say next, when Levy snapped a finger, remembering something.

"Forgot. Brought the evening edition. You're gonna like this, boys." Levy said as he pulled the paper from his jacket, found the column, and read:

"'During question period in parliament, the Honorable Member John Miller gave a speech that, some say, was a direct attack on disgraced MP Franklin Ashfield. The blistering speech lasted a full twenty minutes assailing what Miller called the worst kind of debauchery that prevailed in the House and, in particular, with the governing party. He then went on to...blah blah blah.' Well, you can read the rest later. Anyway, I've heard Ashfield has made tracks for Europe."

Levy handed the paper to Ifan, who gave it a cursory glance, then tossed it on the bar.

"Good riddance."

Donahue had finished his drink and was awkwardly standing holding his empty glass, wanting to stay, knowing he had to head out, back to his desk.

"Well, that's me. Mickey, I'll pay for these."

"That's alright, son."

"He's got a job, let him." Ifan sniped back, not meaning it to sound as harsh as it did.

"Come on now, Ifan."

"No, he's right." Said Donahue, fishing out the coins and leaving them on the bar.

"Hey, before you go," wondered Levy, with a roguish grin. "What happened to the uh…young man, who was with Ashfield? He seems to have disappeared."

"Don't know. In the madness of the raid, it seems he slipped away, nobody knew his name." Ifan smiled and stood to offer Donahue his hand. "Good job."

"Seems like a good moment to have a drink boyo," Doolan said, looking from Ifan to Donahue as he poured four whiskeys. "These are on me."

Standing at the bar with his old and new friends, glasses in hand, Ifan thought of all that had passed between them and where they were now. He didn't have a clue where he was going but hearing the life coming from outside, the Ward in full swing, he concluded he didn't care.

Mickey, holding up his glass said, "what to then?" Ifan looked at his glass, with sentimental eyes, then to the odd group around him.

"Absent friends?"

"Aye, absent friends. Sláinte!" (Gaelic for health)

"Sláinte!"

CHAPTER 36.

Sunday in the city was the one day everything shut down. Nowhere to go and nothing to do. The Sunday Lord's Day Act criminalized about all activities other than going to church or to the Beaches.

With the blessing of the morality squad, the police would hand out tickets in the Ward to the few poor businesses that dared to stay open or incarcerated the rag sellers who couldn't afford the fines, mostly all Jews, of course.

Even the trolleys to the Beaches on Sundays were stopped, so it was a long hot trudge in the summer that always seemed to take forever.

Ifan sat on a bench at the edge of the boardwalk in the shade of a large maple, a few feet from the sandy beach. There, he was able to watch Hélene wading up to her mid calves in the cool lake, her skirts hiked up. Apparently indecently, causing the well-to-do ladies, strolling the boardwalk shaded by their parasols, to squawk.

He smiled, knowing that she didn't give a toss what the rich ladies thought. The beaches were public, they could go to hell, think whatever they liked.

Hélene traced the water with the tips of her fingers enjoying the cool sensation. She looked over to where Ifan was, smoking a cigarette and thought him an awkwardly handsome man. He still had his boyish features even though he was now nineteen.

She waved to him to join her. He shook his head and showed her his cigarette he was smoking. *Some excuse*, she thought.

Getting out of the water and quickly darting across the hot sand to the boardwalk, she brushed off the sand from her feet, plucked the cigarette from Ifan's lips and took a puff. Another scandal!

He loved watching Hélene live in the full knowledge of her body, unselfconscious, alive, and un-apologetic to those who would judge her. If they did, so what? She would just laugh and go on her way.

"What are you looking at?" She said, sauntering up to Ifan playfully, the cigarette dangling from her lips.

"You."

"Me?"

"Oh yes."

She slid along the bench into Ifan, almost knock-ing him off, laughing at her own strength. Or maybe it was his clownish pratfall, acting more hurt than he was. It really didn't matter which, she liked how they made each other laugh.

"I have a present for you." Hélene pulled a small package wrapped in newspaper out of her bag.

"For me?"

"Yes, for you, you dope. Open it."

Ifan undid the string and wrapping, pulling out a new tobacco tin, that he turned over in his hands. Without warning and, not knowing where from, tears welled in his eyes. In the moment, he didn't know why.

"Are you alright? It's just a tobacco tin."

"It's not that. It's… well, nobody's ever given me a present."

"Never?"

"Never."

She put her head on his shoulder, and they sat there in silence for a while, feeling a light breeze coming off the lake.

"What are you thinking?" She asked.

"What am I thinking? Well, I'm thinking, is this girl gonna let me take her away, or should we stay in this city?"

"What do you want to do?"

"I see in the paper they're looking for young men to join the constabulary."

"You wanna be a copper?"

"Beats running away and hiding from them all the time. At least they'll know where I'm at."

Ifan stretched his arms along the back of the bench, and she tucked into him as they watched the waves come in from Lake Ontario.

"What do you want to do, Hélene?"

"Get something to eat."

"No, I mean in life. What do you wanna *do*?"

"I dunno…"

Hélene paused, looked up at Ifan, then out to where the sky and the lake met, becoming infinite.

"I wanna go to school."

"School, huh?"

"Ya."

"Okay, so I'm gonna be a cop and you, you're gonna go to school."

He kissed the top of Hélene's head smelling the fresh lake air in her hair and pulled her close. The two sat there watching life unfold around them, contented to sit in the shade on a hot day.

# Acknowledgements

Thank you to all those who've made this book possible:

Allan Ryan, whose story editing, and patient lessons helped shape this story.

Editors: Elizabeth Campbell & Peter King.

The essays that made up Ellen Scheinberg & Michael McClellan's book The Ward – The Life and Loss of Toronto's First Immigrant Neighbourhood.

The Toronto archives.

The readers who encouraged me to continue: Sherry Roher, Ali Sunderji, Marvin Kaye, and Geordie Telfer.

Also, Christine Sismondo, Andrea Ledwell, Kathryn Exner, and Nick Pashley for all their advice.

Thank you to the bar staff of the Horseshoe Tavern, my note-writing pit stop.

No art is made alone.

# About the Author

Adrian Griffin was born in the Ward area in 1964. He's been a working actor for almost 40 years, as well as an acting teacher and coach for over 10 years. The Ward is his debut novel. He lives in Toronto with his wife Sherry.